THEY'RE COMING FOR MY MATTRESS

[And Other Tales of Life]

THEY'RE COMING FOR MY MATTRESS

[And Other Tales of Life]

Murry Frymer

SAN JOSE

MERCURY NEWS

1999

Printed in the United States of America.

ISBN 0-9653207-3-1

Edited by Ann Hurst and Bob Drews.

Cover Photographs by Richard Koci Hernandez.

Design by Bill Prochnow.

Technical assistance provided by Ed Eke, Raymond Moses, Bryan Monroe and Kevin T. Boyd.

San Jose Mercury News

To the wonderful characters in this book who are
also the beloved in my life:
my wife, Barbara;
my children, Paul, Benjamin and Carrie;
my mother and father
and the astute Hershey, a cat columnist
who contributed much warmth
and perspective to me and my (his) readers.

[CONTENTS]

INTRODUCTION

THE COLUMN ON WHICH THIS BOOK IS BASED WAS CALLED "Murry Frymer at Large." I'm Murry Frymer. I was at large mostly in San Jose, California. Well, it's large enough.

The column began in 1991 after years of writing for the San Jose Mercury News as a film, TV and theater critic. It was a good gig, concluding in 1999, just ahead of the millennium and before encountering any Y2K problems.

"Murry Frymer at Large," like all newspaper columns, was an experiment. You give an old journalist some freedom, a computer, a paycheck, and see what comes. For me, after a career in journalism that began as an editor of weeklies in Levittown, New York, and Westport, Connecticut, after writing reviews and then editorials at Newsday (New York), after senior editor jobs at the Rochester, N.Y., Democrat and Chronicle, the Cleveland Plain Dealer and the Boston Herald American, what came was a point of view. I pondered the life I had led and was leading, which, to my amazement, was not altogether different from most anyone else's.

I wrote of celebrities and of my mother, of political foibles and my cat's fur balls. O.J. and Monica happened to wander through this piece of history. But, truly it was Mom and Hershey, my dark feline avenger, who communicated best. So they, and not the famous, are primarily revived on these pages.

A small world began to take place three times a week, one in which this aging dreamer told of youthful escapades, hair loss and other regrets. Over the eight years of its run, Mom went from being a Jewish mother of considerable wit to a frightened, lost resident of a nursing home.

The children grew up and left. I never managed to say the right things to them. Instead I shared my insights with Barb, my enduring romance, in front of the ubiquitous television set or with myself alone at 3 a.m on sleepless nights.

And, of course. with the readers of "Murry Frymer at Large." Amazingly, the readers multiplied and shared their lives with me, too. Hundreds, sometimes thousands, of responses answered the tales of the ordinary. They became the friends I never had, and we kept each other company.

The world was good in the '90s, vital, rich, expectant. But the most meaningful stories of any decade are the personal ones that do not belong to any particular decade. These stories take place on a mattress, under a shower, on a plane, in a family home that you will never see again.

They are my stories. And, probably, a lot like yours.

Murry Frymer
San Jose, California, 1999.

THEY'RE COMING FOR MY MATTRESS

THE PERFECT COLUMN

Someday, before I'm done, I want to write one really great column. A column that's like the "War and Peace" of columns. Not that long. But great.

I want to write a column filled with insight about the world today. That will make readers all nod and say, "My God, that column was filled with insight about the world today!"

Somewhere in that great column will be a paragraph that will make you all weep. Not just shed a tear. Weep! You will sit there uncontrollably weeping. And when your lover or spouse comes into the room and asks, "Oh, my darling, why are you crying?" you will hold up my column and say, "Read this."

There will also be laughs. The laughs will come through the tears. And while you are laughing you will reach out to your loved ones and laugh and cry together.

I want to write a column that precisely puts its finger on the solutions to problems. When you read it, you will think about the problem and then, in joy, jump up and say, "That's it!"

It will be a column that Bill Clinton will read and say, "Hillary, come here! I need you." It will be a column that Ross Perot will read and say, "I quit. I'm going to join Frymer's crusade." It will be a column that Madonna will read and say, "It's him, not me, who should be famous!"

Yes, before I am done I want to put together 500 words

that say it all. It will be understood by the young and the old, the wretched refuse yearning to breathe free as well as the fat cats yearning to pollute. The Democrats and the Republicans. The victims and the victimizers.

I am not sure what the subject will be. But it will be significant. Yes, before I am done I want to write at least one column that is significant. Maybe it will be personal. It will explore my deepest depths and find that kernel of truth that makes all mankind (and womankind) brothers (and sisters). It will be a column that is politically correct.

Maybe it will deal with something controversial, such as abortion or guns. Both sides will read it and say: "Of course. Now I understand the other position. How silly and mean I was!"

Or maybe it will deal with bigotry. Bigots will shrug: "Oh, what an ass I am!"

I will be invited on "Oprah" to read my column. David Letterman, listing the 10 best columns ever, will say it was mine 10 times over. Playboy will do a three-page spread on my column.

I want to write a column my wife reads and says, "You were right all along!" I want to write a column my kids paste on the front doors of their rooms with the inscription: "That's my old man! Isn't he neat!"

In Bartlett's new book of quotations, there will be my whole column.

In books of famous utterances, they will list "I have a dream …" "Fourscore and seven years ago …" and my column.

There will be a statue of me in front of countless city halls. A statue that stays remarkably free of pigeon droppings. Pigeons will coo to each other: "Not after what he wrote!"

Women will, of course, be the most taken by my words. "It's amazing," they will say, "to find a man who understands!" But men will be admiring, too. "It really strikes a blow for men!" they will say. Psychologists will say: "Thank you for sharing that with us."

I will be modest about this achievement. "Oh," I will say with a slight smile, "it's just a column."

"No," Mother Teresa will respond, "it is much, much more than that."

The Palestinians and the Israelis will agree on peace, based on the astute reasoning of my column. The Serbs and the Muslims will meet, read and hug. Rush Limbaugh will say, "Well, I'm not going to mess with that guy!" Dr. Ruth will say, "Sometimes a great column is better than great sex."

Yes, before I am through I want to write just one column like that. Unfortunately, I haven't got an idea for it yet.

So while I'm thinking, maybe you might read this. While you do, I just want you to know that I aspire to much, much more. It will be something really great.

Someday.

July 11, 1993

I CAN EXPLAIN...

THE PUBLIC IS GETTING NASTY about the press. It has been suggested that if only journalists would open up about how the press functions it would help heal the wounds (or is that wound the heels?).

Herewith, I do my part to tell all.

Q: We've noticed that you talk knowingly to Gary Hart one day and to Pia Zadora the next. What makes you such an expert on so many different things?

A: Careful, prolonged study. I have at least a master's in everything. And anyway, there is not so much difference between Gary Hart and Pia Zadora. Hart likes younger women and calls himself a reformer. Zadora likes older men and calls herself a performer. You don't need a Ph.D. to follow their drift.

Q: Well, if you're so smart, why aren't you rich?

A: The people I work for are. They are even smarter.

Q: The press has an attitude problem. You take a cynical tone with everybody.

A: If we're still talking about Gary Hart and Pia Zadora, I think the tone fits the music.

Q: Well, why are you always printing people's salaries? The sports pages are filled with stories about who makes how much. The entertainment pages are filled with stories about who makes how much. There's more to life than money.

A: Yes, there is sex. But that often takes money.

Q: There you go again being a smart-aleck. Do you people take smart-aleck pills?

A: Well, that's unfair. We just try to be witty. We want to give readers a chuckle.

Q: You give us a headache. And in your political coverage, I think you spell witty p-e-t-t-y.

A: You are something of a smart-aleck yourself. Anyway, politics is petty. We report what we see.

Q: You can't see the forest for the trees.

A: We also like cliches a lot.

Q: How come the media run around in packs?

A: We follow the hors d'oeuvres.

Q: Like if one of you has the story, everybody has the story. There are lots of stories that nobody covers.

A: For instance?

Q: Well, what's going on in El Salvador? What's going on in South-Central L.A. ? What's George Bush's banker son doing now?

A: For every story there is a season. Those stories are out of season. What's in season now is David Letterman, military bases and Pia Zadora.

Q: Pia Zadora is in season?

A: Well, she's in San Francisco and our travel budget is limited.

Q: You also print a lot of violent stories.

A: Yes. There is a lot of that going around.

Q: But you overdo it.

A: That's because it's being overdone.

Q: Well, I think the press is just not focusing on what is really happening in America. All we get is celebrities and Ann Landers and murder and rape. You think that is what the public wants?

A: Unfortunately. The same stuff is on TV. Except for Ann Landers, and she writes about sex and rape, too. The public that wants a serious examination of the issues is kind of small.

Q: So you think it's our fault?

A: Yes.

Q: So what you are saying is the press is our fault. TV is our fault.

A: Kind of.

Q: That is a real cop-out. Don't blame the reader for your incompetence. The press should write about what is important. The press should present a clear and honest view of the world.

A: You're right. We should. We just have a bunch of cynical editors who are afraid you won't buy it.

Q: Well, they don't know anything. By the way, how come they have you writing a column?

A: I write about Pia Zadora.

Q: Yeah. Say, what is she really like, anyway?

July 5, 1993

DE-MENTED DE SADE

A MERCURY NEWS FRIEND OF MINE, encouraging a visit to the Stanford University student production "City of Refuge," offered this advice: "Whatever you do, do not sit in the front row right." It's good to have friends.

The front-row seat, far right, is something for the Guinness Book of World Records, listed under: Worst Theater Seats in Modern History. More on that later.

"City of Refuge," written by Jean-Marie Apostolides, chairman of the Stanford French and Italian department, is a drama about the Marquis de Sade. It is a show the marquis would have loved.

Now, I should point out that I don't usually attend one-act student plays. Nor, I believe, did most of the extensive audience, which lined up hours in advance of the production Friday night at the "Experimental Theater Lab" on campus. But art will out.

All of the students first had to undergo a check of ID cards, the point of which I couldn't guess, unless a certain age was required. If you knew the magic password, "De Sade is alive," you got in free. All others paid $5.

The "experimental laboratory" was actually a common lavatory, a men's room in a small stone building near the university's Memorial Church. Because there were no seats, the production shoehorned about 50 people per performance into the small, windowless room.

I got one of the better seats on the steps leading down to the urinals. Others — mostly students — sat on a bench in front of the urinals or on the ledge above them, or they stood in the corners of the room trying to get a look. The show lasted about 90 minutes, a very long time to endure sitting on a cement step, a bench or standing. But attention was rapt.

Inside, the audience sat facing a white curtain through which we could see two rows of toilet stalls. Only when the lights came up did we discover a filthy man, wrapped in a sheet, lying on the straw floor in front of us. Obviously many had stepped over him getting to their "seats."

The man was de Sade. He got up from what we learned was the floor of cell No. 6 of the Vincennes prison where he was imprisoned. He approached the audience, stopping just short of the first row. Whereupon he flung off his sheet.

I watched him. I watched the young woman student in the front-row, far-right seat face to face with his private parts, determinedly fixing her gaze on the student actor's face. The young man next to her squelched a laugh. Everyone else was very serious. The rest of us were not to be spared. During the performance, the show presented some other unique dramatic moments:

◆ Naked men and women writhing on the flooded floor between the stalls inflicted various sexual atrocities on each other, including simulated sodomy. All this was accompanied by long, silent screams.

◆ One man urinated on the face of another (using a hidden hose).

◆ Long pins were stuck (in simulation) through the nipples of the women.

◆ A man had pulleys attached to his testicles as he lay on the floor. He appears to be pulled up.

◆ The naked cast then marched on the audience, produced apples from somewhere which they munched angrily and then tossed, half-eaten, at the feet of the wide-eyed crowd.

Yes, there was dialogue, too. Written by Apostolides, the drama is purportedly based on letters written by de Sade. In 12 scenes, de Sade protests his incarceration, graphically depicts his past, goes insane, shrieks and grovels. Matthew Getz, who is courageous in the part, was the principal de Sade. (There are two others.) He is from South Africa, a sophomore majoring in English.

The others in the cast were equally memorable in their own ways. The play was directed by Babak A. Ebrahimian, a second-year graduate student in French and Italian, from Tehran. He calls his stylized realism "Filmtheatre."

For all of you eager to see tonight's performance, you're out of luck. The show concluded a week's run Sunday after warding off a custodian who wanted to padlock the place as soon as he found out what was going on in the men's room. Clearly, the students had a hit that could have run for years. Double performances were held on the weekend to expose as many students as possible. One more thing. There was a musical soundtrack that uniquely combined somber melodies and lively songs, including '30s jazz and pop tunes.

Waiting desperately for the doors to open and fresh air to again invade my lungs, I especially liked a toe-tapping version of "Let's Call the Whole Thing Off."

June 2, 1992

PRYOR CONVICTIONS

Los Angeles

COMIC ROXANNE REESE IS ON STAGE at the Comedy Store, finishing her act. "And now," she says, "a real big welcome for a man who's too legit to quit."

A big welcome it is. The audience stands, claps and cheers. And then, in the corner, he enters. Richard Pryor, the angry, profanity-spewing comic who started it all for angry black comedians.

It's a really big welcome for a man who now looks very little, shuffling onto the stage, holding the arm of his assistant. There is a dazed little grin on his face. He looks like a shy child at his birthday party. "I'm happy to be here," says Pryor, grasping the mike for support as his assistant carefully lets go. "I'm happy everybody sees me alive."

His appearance is a shock. He has had multiple sclerosis, a degenerative nerve disease, since 1986. He appears very weak, unable to stand very long. He is painfully gaunt, down to 115 pounds, and his hair is short. Behind thick glasses, his eyes are deep-set, staring straight ahead. Pryor is here to do, of all things, stand-up comedy. He can't stand up, and what can be comic?

Pryor has always been able to laugh at his plight. In the

past, he managed to wring stand-up hilarity from a near-fatal heart attack. Then there was the infamous free-basing cocaine "accident," whereby Pryor set himself afire and nearly burned to death. His friends call it a suicide attempt. That, too, became part of the comedy act.

Pryor has hardly worked for years. He tried an unfortunate film, "Another You," with Gene Wilder last year. So he's gone back to his roots, stand-up comedy, honing an act at the Sunset Strip's Comedy Store.

"Man, it's weird," he tells the crowd. "You can imagine shit, and then you come out (on stage) and your body won't do it." But he's out there. Other have been coming to pay homage to his courage. It's the indomitable courage that has taken center stage.

"Yeah, everybody thinks I'm dead!," he begins. It gets a laugh because Pryor, 51, is expecting it, but most of the crowd is just staring, their hearts in their throats. "They been calling my house. They ask my maid, 'Is he dead?'"

Pryor tries to loosen the mike to raise it, but he can't. "Death is a mothe' f———, man. It'll come."

Pryor sits down in a chair that has been placed at the microphone. He keeps talking, but he can tell that the crowd is not able to decipher what he is saying, something about a possum. "What's he talking about?" he says with a grin to a face in the front row. He can't see beyond the front row. "I got this disease. It's called MS. If you got it, everybody knows it. It's an embarrassing disease …

"They gave me an eye test. Is there anybody here who can't see the (top letter) 'E'? I can't see the 'E.' There was a little kid. He could read the eighth line. It was embarrassing, man. The bad eyes has a connection to this MS shit." I was walking down the street, and I pissed on myself. My friend —

he says, 'Hey, you got something in your pocket dripping? You messing my shoes.' It's weird, man, when you can't control your shit."

Pryor goes on to tell of incontinence while driving on the freeway, trying to get to an off-ramp, trying to wring his trousers at the same time. Again he says, "It's embarrassing."

He says that a sports car pulled parallel to his, and an attractive woman looked over at him. "I want to make a play, but I can't make no play. She's lookin' over and she thinkin', 'Hey, that guy has pissed on hisself.' This disease is humiliating. This is embarrassing, man."

And now the laughs are more genuine. The man is vulnerable but not pathetic. You can still recognize the comic mind, the self-deprecating humor. Bit by bit the pity lifts, and Pryor begins connecting with his audience. Yeah, multiple sclerosis can be funny.

He tells of his determination to enjoy sex. "My penis won't work, man. It's like somebody told my penis a joke, and it's lying there laughing. My woman — she tries to be understanding, but, man, if a woman can't do her business, she gets an attitude!"

And, then, Pryor moves into more pain, talking about last year's triple bypass surgery. He flails his arms as he talks about his hallucinations while under anesthetics. "My bed is a trout stream. I'm fishing in a trout stream. And then Sister Rose, this nun from my school, is there. And I say, 'Hey, Sister Rose, you standing in my trout stream.'"

Hilarious, no. But Pryor gives hints of the old technique, his arms swinging about for a moment. But then his arms tire and flop to his lap, refusing to play their part any longer. There is a towel next to the mike and Pryor wipes his brow, kidding about his need to do it. When the audience responds, he says:

"I love you so much. I'm here on a stage, and my energy ... that wasn't there ... is here."

"You beautiful, Richard!" comes a big voice from the rear. "Thank you," Pryor says. "You lying mothe' f————."

Backstage after the show, the Green Room is swarming with people. Pryor is seated in the middle of a large, semi-circular booth, looking fragile, exhausted, his eyes darting, then staring. All sorts of people come up to pat Pryor on the back, shake his hand and pose for pictures with him. He looks overwhelmed, vulnerable, caught in the middle of the crush.

Pryor has agreed to an interview. He wants to do it in his limousine as it drives around town. Finally, after about 40 minutes backstage, Pryor is half-led, half-carried to the limo.

"Hello," he says, sticking out a hand. "You Mr. Murry?" Two men place Pryor in the rear seat. Then two attractive young women join us, facing us.

———— ∞ ————

Inside the limo, Pryor tries to relax. But he can't. He rubs his back on the rear of the seat. "The cooties got me," he says. "He gets a terrible itching," one of the women, says.

"Want me to scratch?" I ask Pryor. "Nah. The itch moves. You scratch, it'll go someplace else."

Another woman lights his cigarette — he smokes incessantly — and one hands him some pills. Pryor apologizes for smoking. He has trouble swallowing the pill. And he keeps rubbing his back. "The people tonight. They were so great. They were really into it. It made me feel juiced."

Pryor isn't always easy to understand. His speech is sometimes slurred, sometimes inaudible. He says he works on material about two hours a day. "If I do more, I start arguin' with the paper. But it's nice workin'. This is the best weapon I got —

I can get up on stage. A lot of people can't get up on a stage."

And you still make them laugh, I say. "Yeah," and his eyes light up. "Yeah. That's the gift!"

They're laughing at some serious stuff, I say. "Sure. You gotta make 'em laugh. You know what I'm sayin? 'Cause they cry, there ain't no money in that. There ain't a dollar in that. You gotta make 'em laugh."

I laugh. I say: "Well, your mind is still working."

"Yeah," he says. "Except on Wednesdays." That gets big laughs in the car.

You've done it all, I say, hunting for easy conversation, though I fear it sounds like terminal talk. Hey, of all the things you've done, what gives you the most pride?

"I pulled my little baby boy out. Steven Michael. It's beyond anything. She's (his wife, Flynn Pryor) layin' there like it ain't nothin'. I'm thinkin' they should have a band or something! And the doctor let me cut the cord. Now that's the scariest thing I done in my life — cutting the baby's cord."

Pryor has six children from five wives (he married Flynn twice), some of whom did not leave with fond memories. Jennifer Lee wrote a 1991 memoir called "Tarnished Angel" that was especially hard on Pryor, including claims that he'd beaten her.

Is Pryor, the angry man, gone now? "I hope. I hope the asshole's over with. I see young people who remind me of me. They don't understand. Enjoy (life). Appreciate it. 'Cause it ain't gonna last forever."

Richard Franklin Lennox Thomas Pryor (named for four of his mother's favorite pimps) was raised by his grandparents, who ran a pool hall and the whorehouse where Pryor's mother worked. He served a term in prison for tax evasion. He stabbed a man with a fork, and shot up one wife's car.

Richard, I ask, what do you think about these days, when you've got time, at home? "Death. I think how it's gonna be dying. Then I think that's so far off. No, I'm gonna live a long time. But I think, you know, you gonna be dead soon. No matter how long it is, it ain't enough. And I think my father, mother, stepmother, grandmother, my uncles — they gone. They all gone. I wish my father had told me about love, about bein' in love. He never told me about that. He told me about women. In a man's way. Nobody tells you about love. Understanding. Feelings."

Our limo ride is over. Pryor is in pain. "The pain is a laugh," he says. "It's like God's gift. He said I'll give you pain, but it's like a treasure chest."

Getting out of the car, I search for the upbeat. I say I look forward to seeing him again. Pryor picks up on the cue. "Yeah, Mr. Murry, I hope one day years from now we'll be riding in a car somewhere, and you'll say, 'Hey, Richard, remember an interview we did riding in your car way back in '92?' "

There is a tear, but it is in my eye, not his.

Oct. 30, 1992

THE WORDS UNSPOKEN

JUST BACK FROM THE AIRPORT, sending off one of the college kids. I've been there lots in the last two weeks. Saying hello, saying goodbye. It's the holidays. I do a lot of this. I am one of those middle-aged son/fathers.

That is to say I have a mother (my father has passed away). I have kids. Shifting between those roles can be disorienting. My identity is in the eyes of the beholder.

To my mother, I am youthful. I am given instructions, told to wear my coat. To my kids, I am old, a drudge. I give instructions. "Wear your coat!" I can play both these parts on any given day. Sometimes within minutes of each other. And up until now, I have been managing both fairly well. I just have to be sure who I am, whether the son or the father, and the role comes naturally. I might even think I was good at it.

But lately, something new has been added that I know I am not good at: the need to communicate in some significant way. I bring this up now because the holiday season is particularly distressing for the son/father. Lots of goodbyes.

More and more, at occasions such as this, I get this uncomfortable feeling that I have forgotten to have a real good conversation all the time the kids have been home. We haven't really talked. In the old days, that was OK. We'd talk tomorrow. Next week. But now the visits are more infrequent. And some real good communication strikes me as very important.

When the kids were little, a hug and a kiss were real good communication. Heck, when the kids were tiny, just the way they grasped your hand on a stroll was real good communication. But now they walk on their own and they lead complicated lives that, somehow, they never have time to communicate.

Communication sounds like: "How are you?"

"Fine."

So I talk about Cal basketball, or a movie we've seen. It's all part of "fine." That leaves me terribly dissatisfied when it comes time to say goodbye.

The funny thing is I feel exactly the same way when I go back east to visit my elderly mother. We talk.

"How are you?"

"Fine."

And then there she is on the front porch, watching me drive away to the airport and waving, and I can read her mind very well. She is thinking: "We forgot to talk!"

Now, really, we did talk … some. I told her about her grandkids. She told me about some new aches and pains. But, still, there is always the nagging feeling that we didn't talk.

It's really very ironic. I know what she wants to hear. All the nitty-gritty details of living. When was I happy and when was I sad. She'd like exhaustive information on the sighs, the laughs, the questions marks, the exclamation points. Even the commas.

Amazing! That is exactly what I want my kids to tell me. Not "fine." No, what were you thinking when you did this and what got you excited and what moves you to tears? I want my kids to tell me their lives. In detail. They don't.

My mother wants me to tell her my intimate story, too. I don't.

Now, you are thinking that all I need is John Bradshaw's latest book, or maybe the advice of Ann Landers. Well, maybe. But for me that sort of advice doesn't work. John Bradshaw doesn't know my mother. Ann Landers never met my kids. Experts like this give all-purpose advice for all-purpose situations. There are no such things. So it is left to me to figure it out by myself.

How do you tell your mother your life when you want her to hear that everything is wonderful and happy? And, of course, that's not exactly the way it is, but ... You say, "Fine."

How do your kids tell you their lives when they want you to hear that they are confident and strong and progressing beautifully? They don't want to worry you or create doubts. They say, "Fine."

So we're all fine, I guess. The holidays are coming to a close and everybody is going back to all sorts of individual worries and fears and anxieties that somehow get left out of the communication. But, I guess, we'll get around to talking about that later.

Happy New Year, Mom. Happy New Year, kids. Hope everything's fine.

Dec. 30, 1992

WHEN MOM COMES TO WORK

Wᴏ HAT WITH THE SUCCESS of "Take Our Daughters to Work" this week, I have an even better idea. Take your mother to work. I can imagine bringing my mother to my job here at the Mercury News …

"Sit up straight when you write."

"OK, Ma."

"When do you eat? You've been here an hour already!"

"Lunch is at 12."

"You have to wait to 12? You must be hungry."

"I'm all right. You just gave me a bagel."

"It was very small. Was it fresh?"

"Yes, Ma."

"How come you're wearing that shirt? People here dress nicer than you."

"What's wrong with this shirt?"

"You look better in blue. Do you wear that blue shirt I bought you?"

"Yes, Ma."

"Who is that woman who is staring at you?"

"She's my editor. She wants to know why my column isn't

done yet."

"She seems very nice. Does she color her hair?"

"She's very nice, Ma."

"And she's an editor?"

"Yes, Ma."

"She must be ambitious."

"Why?"

"She's an editor!"

"Yes."

"You know, you used to be an editor!"

"I know."

"Editors get paid better, no?"

"Sometimes."

"How much you think she makes?"

"I don't know, Ma!"

"Is she nice to you?"

"Yes, Ma."

"Some women are worse than men!"

"Mom, I have to get this written! They pay me to write things."

"Not very much."

"Well, you can go talk to them about it."

"Really?"

"No, I was just being sarcastic. I'm trying to concentrate."

"Sarcasm is not nice in a young man."

"Yes, Ma. Ma, why don't you go into the cafeteria and watch them prepare lunch?"

"Eh! It must be filthy. I always keep a clean kitchen. That's the most important thing."

"It's not filthy."

"Maybe I'll go talk to your editor."

"Why?"

"To find out what she thinks of you."

"I don't think she'll tell you."

"Yes, she looks devious."

"All editors look like that."

"I see she has a cleaning woman to clean up her office."

"That's not a cleaning woman. That's her mother."

"Isn't that nice. Maybe you should clean up your desk. Your desk is a mess. I don't know how you can find anything."

"I can find things."

"Who is that ugly woman there walking around like a hoity-toity?"

"She's another mother. She came out of the executive offices."

"Really? A big-shot editor's mother?"

"Yeah."

"She looks stuck-up."

"I don't think so, Ma."

"What do they pay him?"

"Who?"

"The big-shot editor."

"I don't know. More than me."

"They take such advantage of you. Everybody likes everything you write. Mrs. Klein, the butcher's mother, says you're another Simple Simon."

"You mean Neil Simon."

"That's right. You should be paid more."

"I think so."

"I'll tell your editor's mother."

"No, Ma."

"You're a nebbish. You have to speak out."

"Yes, Ma."

"You could have been a big-shot editor. You were always smart in school."

"Yes, Ma."

"Of course, you need hair. Editors have hair."

"Yes, Ma."

"I can't understand how you lost your hair. Everybody in our family has hair. Your dad, God rest his soul, never lost a hair."

"Yes, Ma."

"You used to have such beautiful curls …"

"Ma! I'm writing!!"

"So write, write. It pays nothing."

Come to think of it, bringing mothers to work may not be such a great idea.

May 1, 1993

NEW YORK STORIES

New York

I AM AT A MATINEE PERFORMANCE of "Wrong Turn at Lungfish," at the Promenade Theater, a small off-Broadway house. It's a wonderful seat in the third row center.

George C. Scott stars as a blind, dying college dean, trying to make an emotional connection with a young, lower-class girl who comes to read to him. Seated in the two seats to my left on the aisle are two 60-something Brooklyn-accented women, with shopping bags who, clearly, love the show. They repeat every joke line loudly to each other. The blind Mr. Scott appears to take a peek in our direction now and again.

Near the end of the play, just as Scott has reached a tearful crescendo, one of the women gets up to go to the bathroom. "Ethel," she says loudly to her companion. "Ethel, if it finishes before I get back, can you remember to bring my coat?" Ethel nods. Scott tries to stare straight ahead like a good blind man should, but the woman isn't finished yet.

"I'll leave my purse here, too. So bring my purse!" she says.

The woman marches up the aisle with a glaring Scott watching her every step. Soon, the sad play is over. Everyone is weeping. Except Scott. He comes out for his curtain call with co-star Jami Gertz on one side and the other co-star, Tony

Danza, on the other. Gertz and Danza bow nicely. Scott stares out into the audience.

"Where ARE YOU, you a—hole!" he shouts. "Come on down here and I'll kick your ass," he yells into the darkness, staring uncomfortably close to where I sit. The audience is taken aback, murmuring to each other. Danza pulls Scott off the stage.

As we are walking out into the lobby of the theater, I hear Scott's voice again. He is rushing up behind us, wearing a Mets baseball jacket. Ann Meara, the actress, rushes to greet him right next to me. Scott is still explosive. "Did you hear that? Did you hear that? Right in the … last scene, this broad gives a speech about going to the bathroom! She had to stand there five minutes and talk!!"

Meara embraces Scott, assuring him it did not ruin the show, that he was great. He is not assured. The two of them burst through the crowd and out the front door. When I get out and look for them, they have disappeared somewhere down Broadway.

———— ∞ ————

The Easter Parade on Fifth Avenue in front of St. Patrick's Cathedral: It is a glorious day, clear, breezy and warm. At Rockefeller Center, there is a flower show in progress. The crowds are thick, mostly tourists, with hardly an English word being heard. An awful lot of German fills the air.

But also a lot of Yiddish spoken by the abundant Hasidic families, the men in fancy black waistcoats or decorated black silken vests, the women inevitably pushing baby carriages. The young boys also wear the black jackets and sport the tradition-al long, curly sideburns. The animated German families and the more-reserved Hasidic Jews all pose for pictures among the flowers, well apart from each other. It is a scene out of the '30s.

On Fifth Avenue, there are Christian pageants up and down the crowded street, with clowns and musicians and magicians. One rolling dramatic scene moves up the street, the Christ story with a cast of a dozen. The man playing Jesus, wearing rags, his face made up to show scars, pulls a huge cross up the avenue. He also carries a sign. It says: "Need an agent."

———— ∞ ————

We are sitting in a coffee shop on Sixth Avenue, shoulder to shoulder with a throng of office workers, tourists and international soccer players. It is the very-rushed breakfast time, about 8 a.m.

A somewhat disheveled woman, overdressed for the warm day, takes the one empty chair next to mine. She has the visage and dress of a homeless person, though I'm not sure. She appears to be in unfamiliar territory.

The busy waitress asks the woman her order. The woman replies: "I want a banana split with raspberry ice cream."

The waitress has apparently never received such a request, leaving her confused. The woman reiterates it in a very loud voice. When the waitress leaves, the woman takes out three quarters and places them on the table. She keeps shifting them around, in horizontal and vertical order. She waits. Then, the order not yet filled, she suddenly grabs the quarters, puts them into a pocket in her dress, gets up and flees out the door.

We, too, leave before the banana split with raspberry ice cream arrives. If it does.

———— ∞ ————

Another waitress story: A Sunday morning customer at

Wolfe's restaurant on 57th Street is having trouble getting a second glass of water. The elderly waitress, a gruff type, finally brings it, but she lets the man know she is unhappy with his request. "Try to stay sober on Saturday night," she huffs and hurries on.

The man is clearly embarrassed. "What the hell is she talking about!" he says looking at me. "I don't drink. What sober?" He gulps his water and leaves.

———— ∞ ————

A city traffic sign on 8th Avenue: "No stopping! Not for 30 minutes. Not for 15 minutes. Not for 5 minutes! No stopping!"

April 7, 1993 – June 4, 1996

DON'T ASK, DON'T CARE

My cousin Boomie was a soldier. He was stationed in New Guinea during World War II, and he wrote me long letters about the war. He wrote of fierce combat in the jungles and the desperate battles there. It was tremendously exciting, and each letter was a major event in my young life.

Once he sent me an impressive jungle knife that I kept for years, showing it off to wide-eyed young friends. I was very proud of Boomie and raved about him to my childhood pals. He was my hero, fighting the enemy, protecting my country.

I didn't know until I grew up that Boomie was gay. By then he was a character actor and bon vivant around Hollywood. For a time he was a script assistant to Jack Lemmon. During that time I ran across my cousin late one night at the Waldorf Astoria in New York while Lemmon was filming "The Out-of-Towners."

I was there to interview Lemmon and found Boomie in the midst of a boisterous cast gathering, regaling the crowd. That was Boomie. He was always the life of the party, a warmhearted, funny man, overly theatrical at times, but generous and empathetic and talented.

His flamboyant manner could not have failed to arouse suspicion during his Army days. But the Army needed everybody. You didn't ask a man about his sexual orientation when you needed him to put his life on the line. And Boomie did that, along with the thousands of other gays in the military. No questions asked. Later, when I served my own two years in a peacetime military, I met other gay men, all closeted. It was not something anybody talked about.

Nor did it seem to matter. After you got to know men in your unit, you made your friends or enemies on such grounds as personality and intellect and friendliness. Maybe educational and hometown backgrounds were involved. The color, religion or sexual ID disappeared. I was not aware of what private social lives were being pursued. I was primarily concerned with my own.

I remember that in the miserable eight weeks of my basic training in the boonies of Arkansas, I once heard some anti-gay derision directed at me, maybe because I spoke in complete sentences. But then good-ol'-boy Sgt. Flowers put his arm around my shoulders and told the rubes that he had been in combat more than once and if there was any guy in the unit whom he trusted to fight by his side, it was me. That impressed even me. My valor had been validated.

Nowadays, this gays-in-the-military debate seems terribly phony. Boomie was no danger to anybody when he served — except to the enemy troops he was fighting. It is insulting at this stage, after so much military history, after so many bloody wars, to pretend otherwise.

The debate is phony because society — including the military — is an amalgam of all kinds of sexual orientation. A significant portion of any society is gay, even if there are still large populations that are uncomfortable with the notion. There are gay generals and gay chaplains and gay entertainers who perform for the troops. There are gay sergeants and lesbian officers. That is true in the United States as well as elsewhere.

Many of our Western allies have no strictures against gays in any part of society, including the military. Why should we? Why the denial here?

To have asked Boomie to risk his life in combat, to endure the hardship of four wartime years, and then imply that he was unfit to serve is vicious hypocrisy. To say he could serve so long as he kept his lifestyle "hidden" is garbage — Boomie was who he was. He couldn't be John Wayne.

(Wayne, by the way, never served in the military. And, piling irony upon irony, many of the actors who portrayed soldiers in the multitude of heroic war movies were, we know now, gay — such men as Tyrone Power, Montgomery Clift, Rock Hudson and others.)

To say, under the new rules, that gays cannot engage in "gay conduct" is idiotic. Gay conduct is no more or less perverse than heterosexual conduct. And heterosexual conduct, as we well know, can run as out of control as gay conduct.

What of the thousands of Vietnamese children fathered by straight U.S. GIs in that conflict — children who have been rejected by their own society and their American fathers? If there is a gay problem of that proportion, I am not aware of it.

What about the recent Tailhook scandal, wherein male Naval personnel harassed female Naval personnel with impunity? If there is a gay sexual harassment case of that severity in our military, I am not aware of it.

Obviously, as in every other corner of our lives, it is the individual men and women who must be judged. It is not our sexual orientation but our personal character that establishes our behavior. Yet the military not only holds onto its bias, it also makes of it a virtue, apparently supported by a U.S. Congress that itself openly includes gays. No amount of reason and evidence can win the day. Even the president, who admits he knows better, feels he cannot sustain a simple order outlawing the bias.

But that is the short-run present. The times — whether Gen. Colin Powell and Sen. Sam Nunn will admit it — are finally changing. I'm not worried about the military future of our gay and lesbian soldiers. When combat beckons, we need anyone who can carry a gun.

This week, there is a totally non-controversial hearing under way, to select a new justice for the Supreme Court. The fact that Ruth Bader Ginsburg is a woman is getting little debate. The fact that she is Jewish seems utterly non-controversial.

Gays may well be the last U.S. minority against which bias is still openly acceptable. But it won't be for long. In fact, we will begin to forget the identity once we lose our fear of it. This nation is committed to equal opportunity for all, and when all the fear and bias and anger subside, that goal will supersede all others.

It is, along with other American ideas, one of the goals for which Boomie fought. And he did OK. We won the war.

July 22, 1993

DIVORCE AT 96

AGED WOMAN: I want a divorce, your honor.

JUDGE: Divorce? Really? How old are you?

WOMAN: 96, your honor.

JUDGE: 96? How long have you been married?

WOMAN: 64 years, your honor.

JUDGE: 64 years? And you want a divorce? Now? Why?

WOMAN: Enough is enough!

There is recent evidence that married couples are divorcing at later ages.

It is not unusual anymore for couples with more than a quarter of a century of marriage to seek a divorce.

I note that Art and Ann Buchwald, after 40 years of wedded bliss — or not — are now seeking a divorce. Apparently, enough is enough.

All of this tends to be confusing to at least one member of the couple, and I have a hunch it's the dumbfounded male.

For most men, after they have been married two or three years, they get sort of used to it. They may or may not be madly in love, but they are deeply in marriage. It becomes a state of mind, a way of thinking, an enduring place. But men and women don't age alike.

As men become more dependent (on her), women become more independent (of him), especially in this age of feminism and twin careers and exercise. That latter thing is important. Lots of women tend to look pretty good at 50. They are financially independent and trim, too. That couch potato over there is talking retirement. It is definitely a time for reassessment.

Now, how do I know all this? Careful research, my friends. Indeed marriages are as different as the people in them, but I note certain similarities that I have been able to carefully deduce.

For example, she has lots of friends. He hasn't made a close friend since his Army (or college) days. She likes to do lots of things with other women. He never does anything with other men, except talk shop over coffee in the office. She reveals all sorts of things to her woman friends (who, you may have heard, are "non-judgmental"). He reveals nothing, not even to her.

When She goes to friends with problems, they listen. For hours and hours. For days and days. When She goes to him with problems, he "solves" them in two minutes and goes back to his newspaper.

She seeks intimacy through shared "feelings." He seeks intimacy the old-fashioned way. Here, too, it takes about two minutes. She dyes her hair. He loses his. She goes to movies to cry. He goes to movies to laugh. She thinks endless football games are a waste of time. He thinks the same about soap operas.

She gets bigger raises than he does. Politically, she is a feminist. Politically, he is a cynic.

She joins clubs, volunteer groups, interests groups. He plans to write a novel. She goes back to college, getting one degree after another. He plans to write a novel.

She says things like, "How come you don't have any men friends?" He says he does, but they are all 3,000 miles away and he has lost their addresses.

She thinks he is getting more conservative as he ages. He thinks he is getting wiser. She hates cooking. He does, too, but he loves eating. She has lost the directions to the kitchen. He has begun a high-fiber diet, eating only cold cereals. When he can find milk.

She shops a lot. He grumbles a lot. She has heard everything he says before. He doesn't ever hear a thing she says. She gets telephone calls from friends. He gets telephone calls from charities.

She reminds him of her mother. He reminds her of his father. She drives the newer car. He is in charge of maintenance.

She thinks they should communicate more. He doesn't answer. She thinks people should "share" more. He doesn't answer. She thinks she knows why the Buchwalds are getting divorced. He doesn't. He will.

Nov, 11, 1992

MEMORIES OF A PAST LIFE

I DON'T GET BACK TO THE OLD NEIGHBORHOOD much, but a big family wedding will do the trick. We had one in Cleveland last week. East-side suburban Cleveland, over the hill. The place with delis, kosher butcher shops and well-tended lawns. It doesn't change much.

Well, it was wonderful. And it was nostalgic. And, surprise, that old gang of mine is … old. That part of it is, I suppose, a little bit sad. All the memories I have are of young, silly people I knew in high school and now they stand there in the boisterous wedding party, heads kind of cocked to the side with a sort of sheepish grin, saying: "I bet you don't remember me."

In some cases I don't. In some cases I remember someone by the same name who I cannot possibly connect with the elderly fellow standing in front of me. There is Al. Al used to be very tall, or what we used to consider tall. Six-two-ish. He was center of our high school basketball team and all-city in football. He was very impressive in high school.

Now he doesn't seem tall at all. He wears bifocals and seems to stoop a little. "I got out of sports," he says. "I didn't want some lifelong injury. It's not worth it if you get hurt."

So what has he done since? "Selling," he says, without telling me what. I guess it's the art, rather than the object.

"I hear you're still a newspaper writer." Yes, I say, still.

"Still" sounds like a very long time. "Yeah," he says. "I used to read you in the Torch. You were a good writer." The Torch was the high school paper. I was the editor. I used to write articles about Al. Al was the star.

And, for a moment, that's all there is. That's his life story and mine. Doesn't sound like much. But then I see my adult kids wandering around, and I present them like Pulitzer Prizes, to be admired and lauded. And Al tells me about his kids, mentioning college degrees and careers. We shake hands warmly. We've succeeded at something.

Hey, Al, I say, it's really great to see you, and I mean it. I smile into his eyes, and he smiles back into mine. For a moment, I feel closer to him than I ever did. I feel close to a lot of these people. They knew me when. When life was just over the horizon and full of spectacular possibilities. We shared that innocence and naivete, and that is a bond never really broken. They remember me with hair. And I remember them thin.

There is my cousin Frieda standing there awaiting a hug. She and I once shared the same dream — to be songwriters. The big moment in her life came when she submitted a song to a radio-network musical show contest, and it was picked as one of the top 10 entries. She asks me if I remember that. I say I do.

There is the father of the bride, an aging attorney, obviously much older than I. He says he remembers me from high school, too. I blink.

There is the bride, a lovely, tiny girl who is marrying my nephew. My nephew grew up while I was away, and I am not sure I really know him.

There is my mother, now 86, whose face always betrays the emotion she is feeling. It somehow has not aged the way her body has. The blue-gray eyes are still those of a young girl. My mother is an entertainer at heart. She sings old songs with a heartfelt tremolo, amazing and delighting the crowd. "Enjoy Yourself/It's Later Than You Think ... " "I'm Gonna Live Till I Die." "How Much is That Doggie in the Window?" Quite a repertoire.

Mom is surrounded by doting family and yet, often, she seems rather alone, seated there, lost in her thoughts. Dad died years ago. She wishes he were here this day to share the joy, the wonder of it all.

There is my little kid sister. Still little, no longer a kid. One of her friends comes over and tells me a secret, that my sister used to collect clippings of everything I wrote in college and was so, so proud of it all, bragging about me to her friends. I never knew that.

There are other nephews. And there is my wife standing beside me. And I feel blessed. Somehow, my life journey has taken me away from all this. That's how I planned it. I had always wanted to escape the neighborhood, to go off to places more glamorous, more exciting. Now, back home, I am surprised at the warmth of it all. The memories. I've always been a little afraid of memories, and yet here, dancing with my wife to a '50s ballad, surrounded by more family and friends than I knew I had, it is more appealing than I would have believed.

"Murry," comes a voice from the back. "Do you remember me?" I turn around. Yes, yes I do. It's me that I had forgotten.

Oct. 21, 1993

LADY CHATTERLEY FRYMER

D~ROPPED IN TO SEE MOM~ in Cleveland on the way
back from New York. The big news is that the "Lady Chatter-
ley" affair — as I call it — is over.

I haven't wanted to mention this earlier, but, yes, Mom was
close to her gardener. His name was Walter and he had been
doing the gardening at our house as long as I can remember,
long before my dad died.

Walter really wasn't a gardener. He did odd jobs. Or in his
case, he did jobs oddly. As I remember, I couldn't imagine why
anyone would hire Walter since the jobs he was supposed to do
never got done. And, indeed, at places like Cele's dry cleaners
at the corner where he was supposed to clean up but didn't, he
got fired a lot. And rehired. Walter needed the work.

Anyway, Walter kept getting the work at our house. His job
was to cut the grass, using the heavy push-mower we had —
circa 1940 — that really required a mule. Walter did his best, I
think. But once he got into his 90s, he slowed down. My
mom is 86 and every time Walter came over to do the grass,
she would help out. She would hobble out of the house and,
by hand, tear out the grass that Walter missed. She tore out
most of the lawn. And in the fall she swept up the leaves that
Walter missed. Walter missed an awful lot, but as I say, he was
already 90 or 91 and his vision was bad.

After Walter was finished doing the grass, and after my mom was finished doing what Walter missed, he would come into the house for lunch. That was really why Mom kept him on. My mother loves to cook, but now with her kids grown up and gone, and now with my dad gone, well, she just doesn't have anyone to cook for. So there was Walter, who would come into the house and gulp down everything in sight. Walter loved my mom's cooking. He even took a bag of goodies with him when he left.

Mom had another reason for keeping Walter. He was someone to talk to. My mom is hard of hearing, so talking is what she does best. She does not require or appreciate response. Walter was hard of hearing himself so he didn't mind my Mom rattling on for an hour or two. And, bless him, he almost never spoke. In fact, I don't recall what his voice sounded like.

Every week or so — whenever he showed up — my mom would talk to him about various and sundry topics that were on her mind. She would discuss choices she had to make, like whether to move to a smaller place or stay in the old house. Walter kept slurping in the food, staring straight ahead, unmindful of anything but what was on his plate.

Year after year, I would ask my mother why she would hire an 88-, 89-, 90-year-old gardener and then do his work for him. And then feed him. And then pay him! She just said that Walter had always done the grass and, apparently, always would. My dad had hired him and he was a link to that past.

Then there was a crisis a few years ago when my mom fell in the kitchen one day and broke her hip. She went to the hospital and took a long time to recover. I was home trying to help out for a few days when Walter came over to do the grass. My mom got very excited. Walter coming over was something special. When he finished cutting the grass — sort of — he came in for lunch.

"Mom," I yelled in amazement, "you can't make him lunch! You can't even walk. You can't move!" But my mom had no intention of letting him go home unfed. She grimaced and hobbled and somehow managed to cook up a meal. I was very angry with her, but she was a woman on a mission.

Walter consumed it all at the table, totally unaware or uninterested in what pain my mom had gone through to cook up the food. Mom just talked. Walter just ate. Mom packed up a bag of leftovers. And Walter left. Without a word. I fumed, but well, Mom never did listen to me, even when she could hear. Actually, I think Walter would still be working for Mom now, but there was a really bad winter in Cleveland this year. In addition to his non-gardening, Walter had always tried to shovel out the driveway after a snowfall, even though Mom has no car and really didn't need the job done.

But this year, it just kept snowing and snowing in Cleveland. I think Walter just looked up at heaven one day, sighed, and decided that God was telling him to retire. And so he did. It upset Mom, I think. I asked my mom about Walter when I was home. She said she didn't know what he's doing these days. Or where he was eating. "He's an old man," she said sort of wistfully, staring out the window.

I wouldn't really be surprised if Walter showed up again one day. Jobs this good are not easy to find.

April 19, 1994

HELLO, LIFE

My DAUGHTER, CARRIE, is graduating from college this month. Naturally, being an At Large columnist with a wide view of the world, I expected to be invited to make the commencement address. However, the invitation has not yet arrived, and time is running short. That leaves me with a wonderful speech and no bright-eyed assemblage of graduates to which to deliver it.

My gracious editor, noting that there was some extra space in today's paper, has agreed — after some urging — to run it, unless, she says, we can sell another ad.

———— ∞ ————

My dear chancellor, members of the board, members of the faculty, graduating class … (I pause here and look thoughtful). Thank you for inviting me to speak here today.

It has been a number of years since I've been in this kind of setting, seated out there where you are. I can't quite recall who gave the commencement address at my own graduation or what, exactly, was said. I remember that Arthur Miller, the playwright, was given a honorary degree at the ceremony and I, an English major, vowed right then and there to write a play that was better than "Death of a Salesman." Also, I vowed to wed my generation's equivalent of Marilyn Monroe. Only the latter has come true. (Small wink at my wife in the first row who is burying her face in her hands.)

In preparing this speech, I got to thinking about where life has taken me. I must admit that there have been surprises. As one prepares for the dance of life (nice phrase), you intend to do the leading. After a while, it is all you can do to keep up with the music, and then they go and change all the steps on you.

So I suppose life is a matter of adaptation. No matter what you may be intending today, you can be sure everything will change in time and so will you. (Perhaps I should point to my bald head here. No, never mind.)

I remember when I was in college, I got a syllabus for every course. It may surprise you to find that they don't give you one for the life that follows. There is a reason for that. No one really is smart enough to write one.

Nobody in my time would have told me about computers, or cable TV, or about the collapse of the Iron Curtain and the communist system behind it, or about the Japanese economic triumphs to come. (I remember when I bought my first Toyota, a friend laughed and told me he would never buy a "Toy"-anything.)

So as I look around, so many successful men and women are doing work that did not even exist when I first started making career plans. They could not have prepared for all this. But they were adaptable.

And, oh, speaking of successful women. When I got my degree, successful women were those engaged to potentially successful men. I'm not sure how we defined successful men. I'm still not sure how.

But of one thing I am fairly sure, we're probably mistaken. For example, most of us see success as something that all of us can recognize. We can recognize fame and fortune and prize achievements.

You don't have to live all that long to realize that we're wrong. Most achievements don't win prizes. Most of the really successful people among us are unrecognized. We don't know their battles, so we don't know their triumphs. We don't know the defeats, so we can't appreciate the endurance. But that is a good part of success. Life is a fairly anonymous trek along some wide boulevards and lots of dark alleys. A lot of the time you travel alone and you are scared. The victories and defeats are tough and yet they are not covered on CNN and no one weeps or cheers. Except maybe for one or two or three people. A husband or wife. A couple of kids. But don't expect consistency. Husbands and wives seem to come and go. The kids do, too, searching for identity apart from yours.

Am I making it all too grim? It's not. Not necessarily. The older I get the more I appreciate another playwright, Thornton Wilder, who understood that life is not in the headlines, but in the agate type. The joys come in the most common experiences — everything from a good breakfast to a beautiful day, to a romantic kiss to the birth of a child. It doesn't get any better than that. And, surprisingly, those experiences and millions like them are available to all of us.

Oh, but I'm getting ahead of myself and most of you. I guess a lot of you might say that philosophy is nice, but where can I get a job? And some of you might say, I've got a B-plus average, what do I do with that? Well, I'm here to tell you: I don't know.

I had a B-plus average and I'm proud of it. Most of the people I've worked for had C-minus averages, and some of them worked for people who dropped out of high school. That doesn't mean the B-plus wasn't worth it. That's another thing you learn. Achievements can have worth without a big payoff. Most achievements are like that.

So I guess what I'm trying to say as I look around today is this: It is a beautiful day. That may well be the most memorable thing about commencement. That and the fact that you are all young and you've got friends and family who think the path here was worth the money and effort.

One of you might well write a play better than "Death of a Salesman." And one of you might well marry your generation's equivalent of my wife. That will bring satisfaction.

But most of you will succeed quietly and privately. And it will be real and worthy of lots of pride.

(Well, I've just had a realization. I realize I am making this speech not to you, but to me. You, I know, would rather have heard from Robert Redford. But me, I kind of enjoy hearing from me. Maybe that's what commencement speaking is all about. It is interpreting X number of years of head-butting into something wise and wonderful. That, being the case, maybe you should pass on all this, go out and find your own clues.)

I'll tell you one thing that is true and that is from the heart. I envy who you are and where you are. Everything you learn from here on out will serve to define you and the life you have led. But know this — this is a beautiful place you're at. Today. Right now. Right here.

At this point, I expect, the audience, unable to contain itself, cheers and I am carried out of the gym on the shoulders of the class valedictorian and the chancellor. My wife and daughter beam at each other with great pride.

June 6, 1993

I LUV U DADDY

NOT LONG AFTER MY FATHER'S DEATH, while rummaging through his papers, I was surprised to find that he had saved all of the Father's Day cards I had given him over the years.

Most were from my childhood. They were the typical "You Are the Best Father in the World" cards, signed or scrawled with a "Love, Murry" at the end.

I was sort of surprised to find the cards since none of them contained anything more expressive than that. My father was not a particularly sentimental man, certainly not overtly. The cards said nothing much. Except "Love, Murry." Well, I must admit that with three kids of my own, I also have a small collection of Father's Day cards. I especially like the ones from the youngest years, on which the message in crayon says: "I Luv U Daddy." I find it is very hard to casually toss a card like that away.

It is much easier to discard all the ties I have been given over the years. And the pen-and-pencil sets. And the cuff links. But the unique things, such as a misshaped coffee cup with a sculpted profile of me, are kept. The cup was made in school by avid little hands that I remember well and was offered up to me with great pride of artistry.

The point of all this is to spill the beans about fathers, especially the stoic, unexpressive, unemotional ones, which is to say all of us. While brushing the emotion off, we tend to remember every small loving act and word. We may pretend not to. We don't want to admit to mushy feelings, which we have always known instinctively are not manly.

Moms don't have to be manly. They can admit to feelings. They have no trouble with rewarding any hug and a kiss with an appreciate smile, a glow, another hug. Dads get awkward. But, secretly, they have such moments burned into their souls and derive nurture from them for all the days of their lives.

Some women, totally misunderstanding the role that sentiment plays in men's lives, will offer all-too-familiar therapeutic advice about feelings. Don't be afraid or ashamed to show your feelings, they will tell the men in their lives. But that is way off base. Men are not ashamed to show their feelings. They simply do not "share" them. Feelings of this sort of very personal. Men know they have them. But they do not put them on display.

Then along comes Father's Day. Every dad will grumble and say that he thinks days of this sort are dreadfully commercial. Hallmark thought it up to sell cards, he says. He urges one and all not to waste time buying gifts. When pressed, he will admit that maybe he could use some underwear. Or socks. Socks are good.

Lunch is also good, since he will pick up the check. He feels manly doing that. But there are occasionally Father's Days that offer up truly memorable gifts. There is the memory of three little kids shouting their good wishes and then pouncing on Dad at one time and rolling around the sofa.

There is the memory of getting a balloon with a cartoon of Dad on it from a shy tyke. There is the memory of a card from a college kid trying to be sincere, saying, "I really do appreciate everything you've done for me."

Well, I say with a smile, now I've got it in writing.

And then there is the most remarkable Father's Day gift of all. It was the birth of my first child, which happened right near Father's Day and turned an immature, insecure young boy into this thing called "Father." The little kid offered no good wishes at all, but he looked up at me and seemed to know me, and when I held out a finger he grasped it very tight. I didn't learn till later that all babies do that, which I think is God's way of establishing the relationship.

That first exquisite experience was to be repeated with two other kids. Each time I drove home in a daze, mulling over the word "father" in my brain, liking how it sounded and felt.

So here we are, Father's Day again. I guess I'll get a few phone calls today. A few cards. A few pairs of socks. But mostly I'll get the handwritten words that come at the end of the printed Hallmark sentiment. It will say, "Love."

And so, once again, I'll keep those little missives. Put them in a box and file them away. Just like my dad did.

June 20, 1993

25 AND NOT LOOKING

MY MOTHER CALLED TO ASK why my kids aren't married yet. "They'll get married when they're ready, Mom," I told her.

"I'm not getting any younger," she told me.

"I know," I told her.

"I'm not even feeling well," she said.

"What's wrong?" I said.

"Eh, what's the point of talking," she said.

"Well, you called so there must be some point," I said.

"When you're old, you're old. That's all," she said.

"What's wrong?" I said.

"Paul's 25 already. Does he talk to girls?" she said.

"Sure he talks to girls," I said. "He's 25 already."

"So what's the matter?"

"Nothing's the matter. He talks to girls."

"And that's all? He's never going to get married?"

"He talks about other things. When he's ready, he'll get married."

"And Carrie? Does she go steady with anyone?"

"Kids don't go steady anymore, Ma. They just get married

when they're ready."

"She's not ready?"

"I don't think so."

"They're such smart kids, what's the matter?"

"What does 'smart' have to do with it? Dumb kids get married, too."

"They're not dumb."

"I didn't say they were dumb. Never mind."

"I would just love to see them married. If I could see them married I could die in peace."

"That's what you used to say about me."

"Thank God you finally got married."

"And you still haven't died in peace."

"What, you want me to die?"

"No, Ma, I mean I want to keep you alive. So long as the kids aren't married, you'll live. You have to."

"I would be happy to die if they were married."

"What is this, a suicide pact? They get married so you can die?"

"Believe me, it would be a pleasure, just so long as I could see them settled down."

"And what about great-grandkids? Don't you want to live to see great-grandchildren?"

"How can I live to see great-grandchildren if they don't even get married?"

"We'll arrange it so they give you great-grandchildren at the wedding. Then we can have the funeral the next day."

"Bite your tongue."

"Well, we've had this conversation, Ma. In fact we had it

when I was 10 years old. I've spent my whole life trying to let you die in peace."

"Don't be a smart-aleck."

"Well, I would like my kids to get married for a better reason."

"Listen, if I hadn't pushed, you still wouldn't be married."

"I know, Ma. I did it for you."

"My father, may he rest in peace, told me that all he wanted in his life was to see me married. He was so happy at the wedding. But he didn't like Dad."

"So what was he happy about?"

"That I got married. I was his youngest child."

"He didn't like Dad and he was happy?"

"Well, he didn't think Dad would make a living. He said, 'Tailors don't make a living. Why are you marrying a tailor?' "

"So why was he happy?"

" 'Cause I got married."

"Anyway, he died in peace."

"Who knows."

"Well, Ma, how are you feeling otherwise?"

"Eh, don't ask. I'm not getting any younger."

"Well, anyway, I'll call and let you know when the kids are getting married."

"Eh, you make jokes. But time flies."

"I'll mention to Paul and Ben and Carrie that you're waiting. Maybe it will be a push."

"That's all I want."

"Everybody needs a push."

"Believe me, that's the truth. If my father didn't give me a push, I would be an old maid."

"And if you didn't give me a push, I would be an old bachelor."

"That's the truth. People need a push."

"So if you were an old maid and I was an old bachelor, we could go out together. Maybe to a movie."

"Eh, I can't talk to you."

"I'll call you next week."

"God willing."

"Of course."

"And, listen, say something to the kids."

Oct. 3, 1993

YOM KIPPUR WITH
BETTY GRABLE

THE BEST MOVIE I EVER SAW was "A Yank in the RAF." Tyrone Power and Betty Grable were the co-stars.

I know that's an unusual pick, but you have to consider the circumstances.

It was the only time I can remember being taken to the movies by my father, a hard-working, penurious tailor who never had time or money for such things. And it happened sacrilegiously on the holiest day of the Jewish year, Yom Kippur. That holy day is upon us again next week, and I intend to do the right thing and go to services. That's the way I was taught.

But on this one Yom Kippur, when I was but a child, the most surprising thing happened. My father and I started out for the synagogue, as we did in other years. We walked, of course. On holy days, one didn't drive, and, come to think of it, it would be a few years yet before we owned a car.

The place was Toronto, where we lived in a small, attached home near the downtown, a neighborhood of Jewish and Italian immigrants during the Second World War. Hardly anybody in that neighborhood spoke English, one reason that films were not a particular attraction. My parents did take me to the

Yiddish theater once in a while to see plays that seemed always to revolve around hard-working martyred Jewish mothers who were mistreated by their children.

Anyway, on this day we did reach the synagogue and enter. I took my seat next to my father and prepared for a full day of incredible boredom amid the aged, shawled men, bending back and forth in their prayers.

On Yom Kippur, devout Jews stay in the temple all day without food or other concerns. It is the day of repentance, when God determines which Jews will have their names entered into the Book of Life and which will not. You cannot pray too much or too hard on such a day.

Somehow, at one of the breaks, my father ran into another immigrant. His name was Sam, and he sold shoes. I called him (and would always call him) "the groom" because I had been to his wedding.

Sam was one of my favorite people. A darkly handsome young man with 5 o'clock shadow, Sam always had a smile on his face. Unlike my usually dour father, he was constantly jovial.

It was Sam who suggested the unspeakable — that the three of us sneak away from the synagogue and head over to Loewe's Shea's Theater and see a movie. I cannot imagine what my father thought of such an idea. A movie at any time would have been unlikely. But to go in the afternoon? The day of Yom Kippur, the holiest day of the year?

I do not recall the conversation. I do remember my father telling me secretively that I must never, never tell my mother about this experience. I believe this secret was the only one my father and I were to ever share.

With Sam laughing all the way, we went to see "A Yank in the RAF." I remember the film clearly. Tyrone Power was an

American who wants to fight the Germans and enlists in the Royal Air Force to do it. Betty Grable was his girlfriend. She sang a couple of songs.

I loved the movie. I liked all the war movies, but sitting there between my father and Sam on Yom Kipper was the most deliciously evil thing I had ever done. I tried not to think about God and the Book of Life. I was momentarily inscribed in the Book of Malicious Fun.

After the movie, we went back to the synagogue where we had not been missed. Clever maneuver. I am sure the other devout praying men — women prayed separately — could not have noticed. It was exhilarating to sit there again while those around me could not possibly guess where we had just been.

But it was especially delightful that this bit of wickedness was something I had shared with my father, the man who had taught me right from wrong. Now we were conspirators together.

I never did tell my mother about that day. And my father never mentioned it again. However, Sam, the groom, would wink at me occasionally and laugh.

My father is dead now, and my aged mother lives in another city. Sam, the groom, is gone too. I miss his winks.

With Yom Kippur arriving Tuesday night, I just happened to remember this adventure and realized I was keeping the secret. I think I can tell it now.

I know God was not especially disapproving. Both my Dad and Sam were entered in the Book of Life for a good many years after that day. And "A Yank in the RAF" remains the best movie I ever saw.

Sept. 12, 1991

OH, WHAT
A BEAUTIFUL MORNING

IT WAS SUNDAY MORNING and I got up feeling very good. I don't know what it was. I don't know where the mood came from. But I think I had a smile on my face from the moment my eyes opened. I looked over at my wife and smiled at her. She was in the middle of some very earnest dream scene so, despite a wispy thought, I decided to let her finish. I even admired myself for that.

I got up, put on the red terry-cloth robe she had bought me as a birthday gift and headed into the kitchen. I got the coffee going, then proceeded to the front door where my newspaper and my cat were both waiting. Hershey, my aged dark-brown cat, brushed past me with his usual muttered complaint. For some reason, on this rare morning, I found that amusing.

Back in the kitchen, Hershey, the cat who owns the place, started gulping down his breakfast and I sipped my coffee. Today the brew tasted quite good. I got an onion bagel going in the toaster and sat down to the newspaper.

Nothing in the paper bothered me. Not the victimized feminists, not the assassins in Bosnia, not Lorena or Tonya, not the sports news. You know something, I mumbled to myself, I just don't care who won or lost. Nor could I imagine why I do care on most other days.

I glanced at the comic strips and there was good old "Blondie." Amazing, I thought, how a strip that never varies in its now threadbare gags is so comforting. Dagwood taking a bath. Dagwood late for work. Not funny, really. Comforting.

Anyway, and this is what hit me, I got to thinking how great my own family — my life — was. I mean, my two sons were home from college, sleeping off a late Saturday night, and I congratulated myself for having built a life for them where they felt safe and secure and slept soundly. Take a bow, Dad.

And in the master bedroom, messed up with books and clothes and magazines to be read someday, my wife seemed content in her dreams. And I felt content knowing she was there.

Yeah, that's the word. I felt content. I hadn't just won the lottery. I hadn't just sold a screenplay that would bring me fame. Nothing unusual had happened this morning. Yet, I thought to myself, I am enjoying this, sitting here with my newspaper and coffee, my family close by, sound asleep.

I wondered why I didn't feel this good every morning. Most days all sorts of thoughts — angry, anxious, envious — make their way into my head before the coffee has brewed. They are stupid thoughts, of course. They all pass in time, and then are replaced by other anxieties, all transitory, all getting in the way of enjoying the peace that, for some uncertain reason, I was enjoying today.

Maybe, I thought, I have finally reached an age where I am at last maturing. If so, my wife will say it has taken me an awful long time to get here.

The great thing is having the family. Our daughter in New York was probably already on her rounds, living her musical-comedy adventures right out of every show-biz movie. The others, close by today, would begin stirring soon. They are good-looking people, I congratulated myself. They are all caring people, warm-hearted. And they are all mine. I felt great satisfaction.

In a few minutes, they will begin scurrying about. I will hear stories of this experience and that. There will be jokes and complaints. Every one will grab for a section of the newspaper which, at this moment, I had luxuriously to myself. Maybe I will plan lunch at some restaurant. Hey, maybe we'll go to an expensive place we've never been to. Yes, definitely. I was up for that today. I looked down at old Hershey who, having finished the first course of his day-long meal, was licking himself, contemplating joining the household snooze. And I looked out the window into the small back yard. There stood a Monterey pine I had planted some years back and hadn't looked at much since.

I suddenly saw it again and was amazed at how large it had grown and how graceful it stood, tall, well-formed, ready to shoot up some more. My handiwork. Only God can make a tree, sure, but it was I who dug the perfect hole.

The sun was just starting to break through the clouds. Behind our fence a neighbor's old red barn gleamed in the sunshine. A sole survivor of pre-development days, it provided a hint of picture-book New England I once called home.

I thought to myself: I really want to hold onto this feeling. I have done well in life to feel this way, to have people around me to love. These little ordinary days are the moments of my life and they are good.

I sipped the coffee. Was that a stirring I heard in the master bedroom? Or was that Hershey scrunching down to spend a comfortable morning?

The coffee was delicious. The bagel was tasty. Everyone else was still asleep. And I, the lord of the manor, sat royally contented in my kitchen, awake and inexplicably happy.

Oct. 30, 1994

OUR NIGHT AT THE OSCARS

I DIDN'T GET DOWN TO THE LOS ANGELES MUSIC Center for the Oscars last night. Undoubtedly I was not missed. But one year, as a film critic, I made the trip. Drove my aging blue Ford Pinto wagon all the way to Southern California.

We took the old Pinto so we could take the kids. They hadn't been to L.A. or Disneyland and this looked like an opportunity to combine pleasure with ... well, pleasure.

First, of course, my wife went out and bought a splendid, incredibly expensive gown so that, as she brushed shoulders with Streisand and Close, she would fit right in.

And I got myself one of those fancy tuxedos, including an embarrassingly frilly shirt that the salesman said was "the" thing this year. I think he meant for Catskill bar mitzvahs. I was not at all sure that this dandy outfit was what they were wearing in Beverly Hills.

When we got to L.A., we found a motel in the right part of town, got dressed for our trip to the Music Center downtown, lined the kids up in front of the TV set and told them: "Keep watching, you'll see Mom and Dad pull up right in front and the man will open the door and we will come out and we'll wave."

They were excited at the thought of Mom and Dad mixing with Redford and Newman and so were we.

The kids asked us to pose for pictures. They had never seen us looking so magnificent before. Then we drove downtown.

As we did, I said to my wife: "I wonder if we really will drive right to the front of the Dorothy Chandler Pavilion and have them open our door. I've seen that on TV." "Really?" she asked. "On TV?"

Then we were both silent while the panic hit us. We were driving an aged blue PINTO! There was a dent in the passenger side front!

"Really?" she asked again. "You think I should have rented something?" I asked. "On TV?" she was mumbling.

I found myself caught up in a line of traffic heading toward the Music Center. Desperately I looked for a parking lot I could duck into to extricate myself from the embarrassment I was facing ahead. I couldn't find anything.

Suddenly a little Volkswagen Beetle pulled up beside us and honked. Inside was another man in a splendid tuxedo and another woman in a gorgeous gown. They looked over at us, smiled and waved. "I guess they are taking moral support from our wreck," I mumbled.

We found a parking garage and, pulling madly in front of a stretch limousine to my right, I dashed into the place and parked. We both breathed a little easier. We could walk to the Music Center now. The terminal embarrassment had been avoided.

Well, to this day I don't know whether we would have been directed to park right in front and have a valet open our car door. I think the Academy Awards people probably have a system to eliminated Pintos from such scenes.

When we walked up to the building, though, there were the cars pulling up, valets were opening the car doors and fans in the temporary bleachers cheered. "Are you somebody?" they shouted to the passing celebs in tuxes and gowns. They even asked us.

Finally inside, amid the glamour and glitz, we mixed and mingled in the lobby of the Dorothy Chandler Pavilion with all the amazingly beautiful people who were there. I ordered drinks at the bar, standing auspiciously next to Jack Lemmon. I ordered what he did. Then we stood next to Jack Nicholson in the lobby while he made jokes to some lovely woman and we tried to overhear.

I didn't feel out of place at all. I noticed that so many producers in the "business" are short and paunchy and bald. Some were shorter, paunchier and balder. I looked good. Was it my imagination or did young starlets sidle up to me and stare, perhaps thinking I was, indeed, "somebody."

We went up in the elevator with Walter Matthau, who also had very frilly sleeves on his shirt, and pulchritude on his arm. He winked and smiled. Probably thought I was up for some award.

We had a bit of a setback when we got to our seats. They were in the balcony, way in the back, so far back that we had a better view of the stage by watching the TV monitors near us. We saw pretty much the same show the kids saw back in the motel.

But we were there. And so was our Pinto, which, by the way, had given us 125,000 good miles and deserved, at least, a little respect.

March 22, 1994

26 YEARS A FATHER

TODAY IS THE BIRTHDAY of my oldest child, Paul. He's 26. But this isn't about Paul. It's about me and my coming of age 26 years ago. I knew it was a profound thing for me back then, but it's taken years for me to realize just how profound.

Until Paul was born, I was primarily a son myself, my parents' son. The big issue in my life was the same one that had occupied me from my childhood — what was I going to become? What was I going to do with my life?

My thought patterns concerned what I thought of others. My ethics, my conception of right and wrong, were all based on judgments I made of others.

I was young. I was clear-headed. I was certain. I was smart. I was ambitious. I was fun. I was determined. I was admirable. I was right. I was on my way!

And then on June 2, I was a father.

I knew what that meant biologically, but I didn't know how to apply it to myself. What was I supposed to do with the fact? So I drove home from the hospital and in those very early morning hours, I wrote a letter to my son. The contents were and still are for him only.

But, now looking back, the letter was for me, too. The letter pointed out that something very important had happened to me and I would not be able to look at anything the same way. Suddenly, I knew that what I was going to become had become secondary. What was he going to become? And how was I supposed to help?

My judgments of others also ran into a new reality. Judge others? How would my son judge me?

Yes, I was still young and that allowed me to make lots of mistakes, but not big mistakes. I could not be irresponsible! Was I still clear-headed? Sure, but little bits of confusion suddenly popped up about the simplest matters.

Fathers didn't drink themselves silly at parties. Fathers couldn't be as impulsive as I used to be at times. Fathers didn't speed. Fathers were ... fathers!

And there was a new woman in my life — my wife! This girl — my live-in date, someone to have fun with — was my son's mother. We had done this awesome thing. We had created a person. And now I had to be obligated and committed. I had to be responsible!

"Responsible." "Irresponsible." Those words kept going through my head.

Was I in the right career? Could I afford the right home? Was I really a good guy? I was no longer certain.

Smart? Well, we didn't have much money. Smart guys would have some money when they became fathers. Ambitious? Yes. But I was also ambitious for him. My own father had been an uneducated immigrant from "the old country" and really didn't know the pathways of America. But I did. I knew what it took, how it worked, why it was important to have a few bucks to pave the way.

I was more determined than ever. But right? That previous certainty is what changed the most on June 2 and it has bugged me all the 26 years since.

What was — what is — the right thing to do in so many

instances? We all hunger for someone to tell us that, to come to our aid at all the forks in the road and point the way. My own father had been unable to. And now I was supposed to do better. How? Where was my map?

On June 2, 1968, I went from being a self-centered, self-assured kid to being a father. Today, 26 years later, I am much older, more uncertain, a father of three. I think I am on my way.

June 2, 1994

MURRAY, MORRY, MORRIS. WHATEVER

My WEDDING ANNIVERSARY is drawing nigh and that brings up the annual question: Am I really married?

The mystery has to do with the original name on the certificate. It's Murray Freiman. That is scratched out to make it Murry Fryman. And then the second name is obliterated with the name Frymer etched on top of it. It is a suspicious document, indeed. It is just another example of the problems I have had with my name, problems that others seem to have had, too.

Let's go back to the beginning. When I was born in Toronto, Canada, a mere handful of years ago, the nurse allegedly asked my mother what she was naming me.

My mom, then a relatively recent immigrant from Eastern Europe, said: "Maury." That is not how she spelled it. She couldn't spell. She had only a scant familiarity with English at the time. The nurse assumed that, given my mother's accent, she was saying: Murray. Murray is a familiar name in Canada.

So the name Murray Frymer went on the birth certificate.

The problem was that as a child I never got to see my birth certificate. I thought I was Maury or Morry. When I started elementary school, the teacher asked my name and I answered: Morry. The teacher put down Morris. She didn't like nicknames.

So for a few years I was Morris Frymer, which was often pronounced Frimmer. Then we immigrated to the U.S. and one of the documents I got to see was my birth certificate. It said Murray Frymer.

I was amazed. I had never seen that name before. So amazed that I quickly forgot how to spell my own name. I wrote: Murry. When it was pointed out to me that Murry was an odd spelling for Murray, I assumed it was due to my mother's limited English at the time of my birth.

It was not until long after my marriage, when I was a father and was gathering up all the family birth certificates, that I found out the truth. But by then "Murry" was on all my documents and there seemed no purpose in trying to undo a 30-year mistake. The wedding certificate debacle was something else.

Barbara and I were married after a very short engagement. My mother-in-law, who arranged the wedding, apparently had only a vague idea of what my name was. She told the rabbi: Murray Freiman.

In the religious service, as Barb and I stood at the altar, the wedding certificate was placed in our hands for signatures. I looked at it and blinked. "Murray Freiman?" I whispered. "I'm not Murray Freiman."

"No?" whispered the rabbi's assistant. "Who are you?"

I told him and he reached for a pen in his pocket and tried hurriedly to correct the mistake. He made an awful mess of the certificate, but then got the second name wrong again. I told him about it. He said, in a hoarse whisper, it would be all right, let's just continue.

I said in a louder whisper that I thought it would be nice if since it was Murry Frymer who was getting married that that was the name on the certificate. The rabbi's assistant got a bolder pen with lots of ink in it and smeared out the second name, putting the correct spelling on top of it. By then the document was a real mess. But, to this day, it is the only document I have.

I haven't actually had it challenged in court. But Barb is beginning to say that she might.

Sept. 3, 1994

HOW I RAISED MOM AND DAD

"Happiness is a warm and loving family... in another state."

— *George Burns*

I WAS RAISED IN A DYSFUNCTIONAL FAMILY. But we did-n't have words like that in those days. All we had was yelling.

Actually, in my family I was both the oldest child and the chairman of the board. My parents were East European immi-grants who only picked up the local language (English) after I did. They counted on me to learn all the local ways and then teach it to them. When my dad wanted a new car, he bought one and then waited for me to learn to drive. In turn, I taught him.

If you are familiar with the scene where the father is ner-vously trying to teach his 16-year-old how to handle a car, imagine the reverse. I was the frazzled, fearful 16-year-old teacher trying to instruct my helpless father, a man so short we had to place three cushions under him so he could see over the wheel.

Somehow my father, a tailor whose dexterity was limited to needle and thread, managed to get a driver's license, though I have never understood how. I believe he must have traded a new suit for a passing grade. (Barter was an old-country way, and my dad exchanged tailoring for steaks, home repairs, radios and the like.)

But Dad was of no real danger to traffic. He only drove from our house to the shop daily, a round trip of approximately one-eighth of a mile. You could have walked to the place and back in the time it took Dad to get the car out of the garage. But the car, a great big Oldsmobile, was the family pride. After Dad died, I brought the 9-year-old car to California. It had 6,000 miles on it.

Mom never learned to drive. She, however, had her own expertise. Daily she dispensed food and guilt, both in heaping quantities. The food was the nurturing; the guilt was the bill.

Somehow my younger sister and I managed to survive and even thrive. Everything we did as a family involved my learning the ropes and then leading my parents through it. They, of course, took enormous pride in their new-world son. When I wrote my little short stories, they showed them to their friends. Neither my parents nor their friends could read the language, but they glowed to see the words on the pages.

A clever little retort from me was reported to the entire community, all of whom clucked over the brilliance. Yes, it went to my head, which also was admired for its lustrous curls.

My mother still looks at my head when she sees me and sighs. "Oh, you had such beautiful curls," she mourns, shaking her head from side to side. "It's all from the dandruff shampoos."

Somehow my parents made their way, though I as their teacher feared daily for them. When my mother took a job I was sure she would get lost on the journey and never be seen again. And every time my dad drove to work, I shuddered.

But my parents had their certainties, too. Whatever went wrong in our lives, my dad would just work an extra few

hours, make an extra few bucks. At the shop, at home. Sometime we didn't see him for months.

And Mom would just cook. "Eat something" was the family anthem.

Well, dysfunctional or not, we had our good moments, successes, marriages, grandchildren. My parents were real proud of
me and, in truth, I'm proud of them, too. I raised them good.

Sept. 20, 1994

AND FINALLY, PARIS

WE NEVER HAD PARIS. Barbara and I married after the shortest of courtships. Call it acquaintanceship. It was what used to be called a whirlwind romance. At least I like how that sounds.

Through most of that brief time we lived in separate cities and saw each other in hurried visits. I guess we thought we'd get to know each other better after the wedding. So, after a few spins around the dance floor of a Cleveland temple hall, off we went to Europe.

And there began the honeymoon. Actually, it was kind of exciting and we liked the spur-of-the-moment tone. We were heading for Copenhagen, but Barb sat next to a fellow on the plane who told us that Bergen, Norway, was the place to go.

So we did. The plan, then, was to stop back in Copenhagen, fly to Switzerland and on to Paris for our big finale. Bergen was wet, but comfy. We slept in a big feather bed in the top floor of a bed-and-breakfast and both were great. A church next door had a steeple bell that rang the hours and the town lay at our feet, quaint, chilly, glorious.

We talked of our apartment in New York where we had not yet lived together. We visited shops in Bergen and decided that teak was the way to go. And then on to Copenhagen where it was rainier and gloomier. And our accommodations were not quite so comfy. And on to Switzerland which was beautiful as always, one lovely town after another.

We didn't run out of things to say to each other. How could we? We were just getting to know who the other was. But we had never been together so constantly before. This marriage thing was strange. After all day together it was all night together and then all day together again. That's a lot of together.

By the time we got to Geneva, we were world weary. We dragged our bags behind us and wondered what ordinary married life must be like. And, secretly, that's what each of us was hungering for. Ordinary married life, whatever it was.

The place we really yearned to see and share was that apartment back in New York that we would furnish together. And we longed for the ordinary breakfasts and the ordinary dinners and the chatter of the day.

So one day in Geneva, I stared deep into Barbara's eyes and said, "You know, we could skip Paris." Skip Paris? The most romantic place on Earth?

Barbara, however, nodded. She liked the idea of getting on a plane back to New York and heading for our apartment. Suddenly that seemed the most romantic place on Earth. "We could come back and see Paris next year," I said. "Yes, we could," she said.

And so, strange to tell, we skipped Paris and headed back to New York.

But, as things happened, we didn't get to Paris that next year. Or the next. Instead we had a baby. And then we had debts. And then we had another baby. And more debts. And a third. Ditto.

And there we were in our home on Long Island with three kids and Paris never came up again. Until now.

It is suddenly nearly 28 years after the honeymoon. And to my amazement, an editor greets me and says there is a great story for me to do … in Paris. And I go home and tell Barbara to pack. Just like we had promised each other a few decades ago, there's a honeymoon waiting to be completed. We've had the teak, we've had the kids, we've paid the bills.

And now we're finally going to have Paris.

Aug. 2, 1994

THEY ARE COMING
FOR MY MATTRESS

B<small>Y THE TIME YOU READ THIS</small>, she will probably be gone. Sometime this morning, they are coming for my mattress.

It will be an agonizing moment. I will probably grip the mattress one last time as the delivery man tries to take her from me. I will pat her and smooth her. But they will take her, and she will be gone.

I speak of my foam-latex rubber mattress, the one that my wife and I bought right after the wedding. We have been sleeping on it for 28 years. I had shopped very carefully, lying down for hours in one store after another. For weeks I mulled the benefits of foam rubber against innerspring against urethane. Decisions like this don't come easy for me.

Finally, the mattress salesman said: "Innerspring and urethane wear out. This mattress will stay evenly extra-firm for a lifetime. "Wow," I thought. "A lifetime. I should live so long."

So, figuring that this mattress was going to save us maybe a half-dozen future mattresses, we bought the foam rubber. Imagine, evenly extra-firm for life!

Well, the salesman didn't lie. The mattress has stayed evenly extra-firm to this day. Unfortunately, what the salesman didn't point out was that my wife and I would not stay evenly extra-firm for life.

Well, maybe I should speak for myself. I am what you call luxury-firm. Some of my stuffing has shifted so I am not so even. The result is that we have been looking glumly at our mattress for some time now. "It's awfully firm," Barbara has been saying. "And even," I have noted.

Well, eventually a mattress sale came along that we could not pass up. I acceded. I no longer felt like going from store to store lying down for an hour.

But then, all week, as I waited for them to come take my foam-rubber mattress, I spent each night lying face down on the sweet old foam rubber, shedding tears. The mattress feels so good, so familiar, so firm.

I don't have to tell you that I and my wife and my mattress share lots of … uh … history. The good times and the bad times. My mattress has provided the foundation for our marriage. It has been there to share in the laughs and tears, the joys and jars of many a night.

It's on mattresses that families are conceived. It's on mattresses that we become families! I remember Barbara nursing our offspring on that old mattress. I have pictures of that, not realizing when I took them they were pictures not only of Barbara and the kids, but also our beloved mattress.

If mattresses could talk, our old foam rubber could tell our most intimate secrets. (Well, thank goodness they can't. I would have gotten rid of it years ago.) But mattresses don't talk. They just lie there and give you their support. Year after year.

In weighty matters, their firm strength can be a warm comfort on a cold night. My foam-rubber mattress sure was.

But, anyway, today, they are coming to take her away. (Mattresses don't have a sex, I know, but, as in describing a ship, feminine seems right, kind of nurturing.)

I will miss her. Oh, I know that our innerspring replacement will try to back us up the way the foam rubber did. But a lot of time — wonderful time — has passed now. There won't be any nursing of infants on the new mattress.

So, goodbye old girl. You were a firm friend right to the end. Extra firm, actually.

Sept. 24, 1994

AS TIME GOES BYE-BYE

I HAVE BEEN SEARCHING through newspapers for an important story I cannot find. That's the problem with newspapers. The important stuff isn't covered.

Well, I'll bring it to you and let the investigative reporters do the follow-up research. This is the news: Time is moving faster.

I don't know if this has anything to do with Einstein's theory of relativity. And who knows, maybe I'm onto a Frymer theory of relativity that is even bigger. I know for a fact: Time is moving faster.

Here is the evidence. When I first became aware of time, I noted studiously that it moved rather slowly. I think my first discovery of time was as a youngster. I would be told, for example, that I would be taken to a baseball game on the weekend. That, I noted, carefully perusing my calendar, was five days away.

I figured it out. Five days times 24 hours equals 120 hours. Those 120 hours moved slowly. V-e-r-y slowly. I waited and waited but it took forever for the weekend to arrive.

Over the years, I have expected time to always act like that. However — and this is what I have recently discovered — time is now not like that at all. For example, I may plan to do something six months from now. It may be a vacation or just cleaning the garage.

What happens? I go to bed and wake up in the morning and my wife tells me, without even a sly grin, that six months have passed. I say that I am not an idiot. Only a night has passed. She points to the calendar. And, according to those circles she makes around every day, it really is six months later.

It is even more eerie looking backward. For example, I meet a friend with whom I used to work. He left the job a couple of weeks ago to get married. I greet old Joe and ask him when the wedding will be. He looks at me blankly and then introduces his wife and two kids.

I go home and tell my wife about this strange event. "Somebody or something," I say, "is fooling around with time. Joe left the job two weeks ago and today he is three years older. And he's got a whole family. How could he do all that in two weeks?"

Believe me, this is very serious. For example, we all rely on a reliable measure of time in planning our future. I, for example, have other chestnuts to roast and I have placed those plans within a certain time span.

According to this time allocation, I was going to write my great American novel by the time I was 40. Or 50. Naturally, I expected there was lots of time between decades. But that was before I knew about this new phenomenon, the current time speedup.

Time now moves so quickly that one can hardly make a future plan and, the next thing you know, it has passed. Every week seems to go by in a day. Time is virtually zooming, yet I have seen no alarm expressed over the fact. Everybody is unaware of what is happening.

Is it some diabolical plot? "The Twilight Zone?"

I figure if I can find out who is responsible for the speedup,

I might be able to get back at least 20 or 25 years. I could get started on that novel and become rich before I was 40. I have all sorts of plans I could rekindle. I could get together with friends before they have aged. I could see the world the way I planned.

Whoever has sped up the time — I'm onto you!

Sept. 27, 1994

THE MAN WHO
UNDERSTOOD WOMEN

Please understand that some of the negativity that follows comes from a deep-seated jealousy.

"Relationship" guru John Gray has sold books in numbers that other writers can only fantasize about. His "Men Are From Mars, Women Are From Venus" has been on the New York Times best-seller list for something like 73 weeks now and sold better than 2.1 million copies. Apparently there are countless women who see in him something unique — a man who understands women.

Hundreds of thousands of such women (and not a few men) have attended his lectures, seminars and workshops all over the country, including San Jose, paying hundreds of dollars apiece to bask in his charismatic wisdom. The man clearly knows something.

But he's a slow learner. The wide-eyed Marin-based Gray, now 42, spent nine years as a celibate monk, then decided that his yogi was not God. So he turned to sex and found out he liked that better.

While having sex, which he quickly mastered — he claims three days of foreplay for one grateful mate — Gray began considering how different women were from himself. For example: "If a man respects a woman's primary need to be heard, she will respond by becoming equally respectful of his wishes." And: "When a woman is angry with a man, the most powerful message he can send her is that she has a right to be angry."

Such understanding runs through Gray's latest epic, "What Your Mother Couldn't Tell You & Your Father Didn't Know," another catchy title. Undoubtedly, women, who buy the overwhelming majority of such books, will be pleased. Women in this book are all about love, all about feelings, all about nurturing, all about warmth and sharing and ... did I mention love? Men talk to solve problems; women talk to evoke feelings.

We learn that a woman needs to be touched 10 times a day for her self-esteem. A man needs sex for his. Once a woman lets a man touch her in a sexual way, he will never be satisfied touching her in the nurturing way she covets. "Modern women give too much and feel overworked while men give only what their fathers gave and expect the same measure of support."

What is so smooth in all this is the pretense that all women and all men are alike. That once you understand the gender, you can go right home and be, well, as understanding as John Gray is.

Gray, by the way, is the man who, after having a woman offer herself to him in a hotel room, went home and, he writes, asked his wife whether she would mind if he had occasional extramarital sex. "It would just be for fun," he told her, "and I will be very discreet."

After his wife wept in that wonderful way that women have of weeping when men want to cheat on them, Gray writes, "In that moment, I knew that Bonnie loved me ... she needed monogamy as a requirement for growing in love."

Well, is he understanding or what? And he writes beautifully, even if it is beautifully banal.

Bonnie, by the way, is Gray's second wife. His first, Barbara De Angelis, is author of "Secrets About Men Every Woman Should Know." They divorced while giving workshops together on "Making Love Work." That was because, he says, she was cheating on him with her macrobiotic consultant.

"When my marriage failed, I had to re-evaluate everything I knew about relationship skills," he writes. And then, later, re-married and re-evaluated, he asked Bonnie if she minded if he fooled around in various hotel rooms.

The man is from Mars.

Oct. 22, 1994

HER CALLING IS PHONE SEX

EVERYTHING YOU WANTED TO KNOW about "phone sex" and you were waiting for me to find out: I called Natalie Rhys. She is a "phone sex fantasy performer." She works the phone only part time. Apparently full-time phone sex is exhausting.

Rhys works days in an office as a computer operator, or other office work. At night she likes to curl up with a good telephone.

Being a proletarian, the first thing I wanted to know was how much she earns from her phone career. She said about $15 to $20 an hour — or $10,000 to $15,000 a year. A full-time talker could earn $50,000, but 40 hours a week of phone sex might require mouth-to-mouth resuscitation. As for what it costs the callers, figure $35 to $40 for a 20-minute call — like, she said, "a good meal at a good restaurant." The average call: 10 minutes. But, oh, the telephone bills do mount for persistent, insistent callers!

So much for the economics. The fantasy is in the details. I asked Rhys to ... uh ... begin. She told me that the first thing she usually does for hesitant callers like myself was to describe herself. She's voluptuous, gorgeous, lying there naked on her silk sheets. Well, not entirely naked. She is wearing a garter belt and see-through stockings. I said that was very nice. She said she was kidding.

"Actually," she told me, "That's the description for the callers. It's not realistic." Rhys, in a fit of journalistic honesty, told me she is 47 and not especially voluptuous. I sighed, but went on. Heck, I wasn't paying for this call.

Rhys also told me she is divorced, has an 18-year-old son, and enjoys her work some of the time and is bored some of the time. Just like my job, I told her, only my callers never ask me what I'm wearing (a garter belt and see-through hair).

Anyway, Rhys said her callers usually have a fantasy that they want her to dramatize. "Like they have the hots for somebody in their office but they've never had the nerve to approach that woman. It's usually some woman in a position of power — a boss, a principal. So I make up a story about how we're alone together and everybody else is gone and how I've always wanted this to happen. And please touch me. Like that." I was already breathing hard. "Go on," I moaned. "Well," she continued, "not all the calls are the same. Some are unusual. Like the man who wanted me to be gagged."

"How do you do phone sex gagged?"

"Well, it depends on the fantasy. In this one I screamed a lot, sort of muffled. And groaned. And screamed. In another call, the man wanted me to be a woman with amputated legs."

I was beginning to see the effort in all this. It's like dramatic improvisation. I asked Rhys if she had ever thought of acting for a living, not that she wasn't already. She kind of giggled and said, "I'm not particularly photogenic." I wished she wouldn't keep saying things like that smack in the middle of my fantasy. "But this is acting only with my voice," she said. "It's kind of private acting."

I asked Rhys how she got into this specialized work. She said it was through a friend, back in 1987. It's not easy finding such a job. There are more women wanting to do it than jobs available, she said.

Yes, she is happy in the work. She believes phone sex is a safe form of pornography, provides "an illusion of intimacy," is an aid to relieving loneliness and, at times, is even fun and "energizing." Never, though, a turn-on. That's for the caller. In fact, according to Rhys — who claims expertise in the sex-fantasy field — women are rarely turned on by phone sex. They may like the job, but they don't make the calls.

The more Rhys told me about her job, though, the sadder it sounded. She claimed that phone sex "doesn't hurt anybody," but I wondered if it really helped any of the frustrated, lonely and even sick men who called.

Rhys, who works the phone out of her home, sometimes while making dinner, never tells any caller anything truthful about herself. Not even her name. It is all fantasy, a game. But the callers usually do reveal much that is intimate about themselves; in fact, Natalie elicits it for the sake of the fantasy. When the call is over, she has a modest commission; he has his sexual release. That's the bargain and the business.

Rhys says she also does volunteer work to help people. She answers a telephone crisis line and serves on the board of a Quaker retreat center. I wanted to say something about not getting her crisis and sex calls mixed up, but let it pass. On a call back later to Rhys, her 20-ish son happened to answer the phone. I asked the young man how he felt about his mother's work. "I've never really thought about it that much," he said. "She's been doing it as long as I can remember. It's just a job." And, I mumbled to myself, "Somebody's got to do it?"

Oct. 27, 1994

OUR LOSS OF INNOCENCE

THE REVIEWS FOR THE FILM "QUIZ SHOW" were outstanding, but the box office receipts have been disappointing. Dramatically, it's an exciting, well-acted and thoughtful movie. But I can understand the muted public response. This film isn't about the usual cinematic murder and mayhem. The big crime here is public deception.

Maybe we can add such personal moral or ethical issues as pretense, dishonor, even greed. It's also about being true to yourself, upholding your ethical convictions. It's about what we used to call integrity.

(Hey, do I hear you all slumbering off?)

"Quiz Show" tells the mostly true tale of Charles Van Doren, an Ivy League college instructor and son of a famed author and educator. Van Doren succumbs to temptation when producers of a '50s quiz show, "Twenty-One," talk him into accepting the answers in advance, thereby participating in a notorious deceit. Van Doren wasn't the only one of the show's participants who faked their roles to please the producers. All the contestants apparently did.

But Van Doren, the fair-haired scion of an esteemed academic family — portrayed nobly in the film, almost with awe — should have known better. In the end, when the truth is out, the nation is shocked and he is disgraced.

Well, in fact, I remember it happening in just that way. But if any film indicates the vast moral and ethical gulf between then and now, this is it. Van Doren's lie shocked the nation. America now appears unshockable.

We've just gone through a political campaign where virtually every candidate was accused of lying and, in most cases, that was the least of it. We've got stories on the front pages of trusted priests who molest choir boys, of loving mothers who kill and blame others. We've gone through Watergate and every other "gate" pointing to Washington deception. The president we called "Tricky" quit.

Now we've got adultery in the White House and Buckingham Palace. We've got amiable wife-beating O.J. And we have lived through Iran-Contra and Ollie North. Lying? Do we still make such ethical judgments? How innocent we must have been once upon a time. Now we watch Sally Jesse and Jerry and Geraldo and Maury and find a guest-list of such deceptive trash that you have to wonder how they were dug up. Faked quiz answers? Now we get whole shows that are faked and others that thrive on hypocritical shock values shoveled up daily for an eager sensation- hungry public.

"Quiz Show," in contrast, raises issues that in the '90s seem almost quaint. Did we really believe back then that "a professor" was some kind of superior animal, possessed of impenetrable integrity, who would not be tempted by big winnings? Yes, we did. We thought there were people of character whose honor was stronger than any temptation. They were — we were — "on the level."

Well, now we expect much less. Deception is now as American as, well, quiz shows. In fact, there are few things in the public marketplace that we do trust. We distrust our leaders, our employers, the press, TV, the plumber, the broker, the cops and the guys who fix our cars. Privately we distrust our neighbors, often our families and sometimes, given temptation, even ourselves. Charles Van Doren, after his anguished confession, was filled with such shame, he never again tried to be a teacher. He disappeared from public view and has lived a quiet, unseen life.

Shame? That's another one of this film's quaint concepts.

Nov. 12, 1994

MUSEUM OF US

Back home. It is always the same. I walk the rooms of my mother's house and it is a museum. It is a museum of me, of my sister, of our kids, of our lives.

In room after room, there is nothing but us. Us as toddlers. Us as teen- agers. Us as parents. Us. There are collections of old cards, old letters, old invitations. There are trophies, prizes, medals, newspaper clippings and mementos. All on display. All on us.

My mother is downstairs now, boiling water for coffee. I will hear the whistle from the kettle any second now and she will not because she is hard of hearing. I will go downstairs and turn off the burner. She will say the water was not yet boiling and I will say that it was. Even the dialogue in this house is old. I will sit at the table and drink the coffee and she will offer chocolate chip cookies and apple cake and bagels and everything else in the house. I will decline and she will say, "I don't know how you can drink coffee without eating something." Another old line.

My mother grows older, into her late 80s, and yet her face remains soft and her blue eyes appear as young as I remember them. The body is hunched, the smile still warm. But her look is distracted. Her thoughts ramble and she repeats herself end-lessly. She sees me as a boy, still. The stories she tells over and over — so I will remember them — are of the old country when she had lots of youthful nerve and left for America, stopping for a day in Paris.

"I wasn't afraid of anything then," she says. "I went all over Paris. I saw everything. I was a young girl."

She loves to tell me that. She loves that image of herself. She says, nodding her head, "Your mother wasn't always old." Now she is, she says, "an old lady." She hates that.

And she goes on. She used to be pretty. She has old pictures in old boxes that prove it. I have seen the pictures. People in weird poses, serious, gathered around a table very formally. But she is right. She was the prettiest one.

"So what can you do?" she says. "You grow old."

An occasional panic grips her at odd moments, inexplicable to even her. I see it come over her. She hunches down like a cat, protective. She doesn't like strangers in the house. She refuses to have her old carpeting replaced because she doesn't want strange men — the carpet layers — disrupting her world, messing up the house.

And she is suspicious, too. The outside world has become unfathomable, disturbing. So she sits by the front window watching the traffic and the neighbors and here she feels safe. She waters the plants — a collection of gifts from Mother's Days past — and says how well they are doing.

"The plants are like my children now," she beams.

The plants have replaced the people here. What is not of me and my sister in the house is of my dad, who died some 13 years ago. There are little things, like his address labels, his old pens, his old ties. All where they always were.

The dishes in the kitchen are the ones I grew up with. I remember following the designs with a fork when I was a child. An old knife looks odd. Brought from Europe, it has been worn to a quarter of its edge.

There are calendars of years long gone. There is a receipt for a TV set bought in 1972. There is an old can opener that hasn't worked in years. A plastic table radio, a phonograph that plays records, not tapes or CDs.

I say that the house needs new carpets and my mother says she will think about that. I say that the house needs some paint and she says she will think about that, too. She brings me up to date on who has died in her world, who is ailing, who has moved to a nursing home. She shakes her head worriedly at that. "The old people there are worse than dead, worse than dead."

She tells me that the new gardener is doing a bad job cleaning up the leaves. She has to go out every day on her ailing legs and sweep up, she says. She says the shows on television are terrible now. "Only fighting and killing. They used to have such good stories. Where are all the good actors? There's no Jewish actors."

I sip the coffee and she laughs and says that I always took hours to finish my cup, carrying it around the house until it was cold. She tells me that I haven't changed. I sip the cold coffee and think, oh, yes, I have changed. And she has changed.

Only this house is the same.

Nov. 13, 1994

DON'T TAKE MY WIFE, PLEASE

I told a joke; I know not where.

It fell to earth and died right there.

And now I sit alone and stare,

Bereft of laughter, love and hair.

— *Song of the Lonely Humorist*

I SEE WHERE NEWSPAPER HUMORIST DAVE BARRY and his wife are getting divorced. That struck me as not funny. I write this as a very worried man.

Though I do not know the source of the Barry marital strain, I do know that humor columnists are clearly hell to live with. Yes, I do know. I live with a woman who lives with a humor columnist.

She picks up the paper most days with trepidation. Did the resident humor columnist mention her name in some smirky way in the column today? Did he do any "Take my wife …" jokes? Or did he discuss their sex life publicly, embellished with a series of clever witticisms?

At home she can bear it, stoically. But then there is the business of being recognized in public. Well, actually, it is the bald humor columnist who is recognized. After all, he has his picture in the paper and his dome has become a shiny beacon of familiarity.

The waitresses and salesmen approach with a smile. Then they turn to the humorist's wife. "He must be very funny at home," they say to the cringing woman. The wife, I am grateful to report, says nothing. She takes "For better or worse" seriously. It includes moments like this.

Humor columnists are not very funny at home, no matter how "Dave's World" portrays them on TV. Humor columnists, wound up all day in their avid search for mirth, wind down each night into a fetal position. They make no jokes because there is no audience there to appreciate them. Humorists may like to have their wives in the audience but not be the audience. A wife is a very tough audience.

Nevertheless, it has become clear to me, humor columnists need their wives more so than most men. Humorists are … well, pathetic. They cannot live on past triumphs. They are only as successful as their latest column. If it goes into the toilet, so do they.

Alas, that means they require special understanding. If the joke was about her, they require forgiveness.

If the editor mumbles, "You really think this is funny?" they require new confidence. Conditioned and consumed with the comic's single-minded need to make merry, they require a life. They require a life with an understanding wife. In this feminist age, there are not many who would play the part.

So, I would like to tell Dave Barry that I am real sorry, as I once told the divorced, somber Art Buchwald, too. I hope the Barry split doesn't hurt the TV show. It is, of course, one of my favorites, as is the Barry column.

And I would like to tell my wife I am real sorry, too. For all the past columns. For all the bad jokes. I am really going to try to find some other source of merriment than "the wife." I understand. I empathize. I am going to try.

Of course, there is always an old standby, my mother. She adores the recognition — and even if the jokes are bad, mothers don't divorce you.

Nov. 17, 1994

AFTERTHOUGHTS
ON FORESKIN

THEY WERE TALKING ABOUT CIRCUMCISION on radio. I wasn't paying much mind. Circumcision is a decision that has come and gone in my life. For me and my sons, the foreskin follies were a foregone conclusion. It was ritual. But now, I understand, lots of "experts" disdain the practice, be it for religion or health.

There was one woman on the PBS program who was really upset. She said that circumcision was an attack on human rights, that it was an act of brutal disfigurement, that it had a psychological aftermath that led men to become violent.

She said that for many circumcised men, way down deep in their psyche is a resentment toward what had been done to them, and then as adults they try to get even. That could explain Steven Seagal.

I thought she was going overboard. But then, as one red light turned green, someone said something that really shocked me. "Men who have been circumcised," said one panelist, "enjoy only a small percentage of the sexual pleasure of men who have not been circumcised." I almost drove off the road.

Now I was listening closely. One male caller said that he had been circumcised as a baby, but then had the foreskin replaced as an adult. "And it was fantastic," he said, speaking of his sexual awakening. "All those years," he said, "I had never known what I was missing."

There were more calls similar to that. Testimonials to foreskin. "Don't you see?" said another caller. That's where the nerve endings are." The woman who had spoken of human rights — to nobody's particular interest — now was animated. She chortled that men everywhere were seeking to have their foreskins replaced.

"Parents should realize just how serious a deprivation circumcision is," she was saying, glad to have everyone's ear. Well, she had mine. "Men who have been circumcised have no idea what they are missing!" I let that waft through my cerebrum. Could this be true?

This is the sort of idea that can drive a man mad. How would you like to be told, for example, that your taste buds are defective? That you just don't know what pizza tastes like because you lack a facility for spices?

Well, unfortunately, there is no way of knowing. Sex certainly has seemed pleasurable in my life. I keep thinking: "seemed." But, if these experts know their stuff, imagine what it must be like for non-circumcised men.

Well, as I drove along, I decided to change the station. Listen to Rush Limbaugh, maybe. But my mind wandered. Most men, I mused, even if they have concerns about circumcision, are unlikely to hunt around for their old foreskins. And who wants somebody else's?

Still, I hated to think that life is full of champagne and caviar and I've spent it all sipping Kool-Aid. It's like when I tell a friend I had a wonderful time at Tahoe. And he smiles and says, "Nice, but have you ever seen the Alps?"

It's like when I show an old friend my best column and he

just nods, then adds, "By the way, have you read my 12-volume series on the rise and fall of the Roman Empire?" That's show-off stuff.

Maybe all those guys with foreskins are just showing off. Maybe it's not nearly as great for them as they want us deprivees to feel. That's what I believe. And I wish they'd shut up.

Dec. 8, 1994

RICH REMEMBRANCE

MY PARENTS NEVER WENT TO RESTAURANTS. Never. Restaurants were foreign to them, considered a supreme luxury.

Instead, my mom's kitchen was the equivalent of a Catskills resort. There was always something cooking in the oven, a sponge cake cooling on the table. The smells were rich. The menu was glorious. We ate like kings.

My wife and I, however, now eat at restaurants quite a lot. We do not consider restaurants a luxury at all. Our home kitchen is devoted mostly to easy-to-fix health foods. My wife and I work and have no time for cooking.

My parents never traveled very far by car. That would be expensive. Gasoline was not to be wasted. My father didn't even own a car until he was in his mid-40s and then he drove a mile or two a day. In all his life, he never accumulated 10,000 miles. My parents traveled by bus mostly and on outings to the beach or wherever, we carried our food with us. Trips were often adventures, to be recounted later with laughter.

My wife and I have two cars and they are a necessity, not a luxury. We drive in air-conditioned comfort, safe and sound in our private surroundings, listening to the stereo. We spend half our lives in our cars, in our private surroundings, listening to the stereo.

What did my parents do for fun? They went to weddings. To confirmations. There was always a gathering of family and friends. Every weekend, it seemed, we dressed up to go to somebody's celebration.

My parents were members of immigrant associations. Everyone came together frequently, for help or happiness, sharing in the births, deaths, weddings and bar mitzvahs. It was a community of people who cared for each other.

My wife and I are not immigrants. We live in a larger community, an anonymous one. We rarely see our relatives, the second and third generation of whom are scattered across the land. I fear that in another generation, we may not know who we are.

My parents did not buy a lot. Times were tough, money was scarce. Instead they bartered. My father, a tailor, would sew something for the shoestore owner who, in turn, provided us with shoes. My father did alterations for the butcher who came by with fine cuts of beef. We lacked for nothing, or at least so it seemed. And we got to know the shoestore owner and the butcher quite well.

My wife and I, on the other hand, buy quite a bit. My wife likes to shop and our closets are full. We should be friends with the people at Nordstrom, but we are not.

People were always dropping in unexpectedly at my parents' house. They would bring over some pastry and, in turn, share in our desserts. There was coffee, conversation, laughter and talk. It was the daily entertainment.

For my wife and me, entertainment is a concert or play or movie as far away as New York, something my own parents could not possibly afford. Our entertainment costs quite a bit more than my parents'.

What is the point of these comparisons? My parents were poor, though I did not know it at the time. My wife and I are comfortably middle-class. We are able to afford much that my parents could not.

So why then, when I think of my parents' life, do I remember a time that was rich? And why, with our current gains, do I feel such losses?

Feb. 25, 1995

MY BEST IDEAS ARE ALL WET

IDO MY BEST THINKING IN THE SHOWER. I don't know why it is. Put me under a steady stream of hot water and my thoughts flow freely, too. I think it's because the hot soaking puts me into a very positive state of mind. After a few minutes, ideas that didn't come earlier are suddenly abundant. My IQ goes up as the water comes down. I grow imaginative, clever, profound. I just wish I had some dry paper to write all the good stuff down. No doubt about it, in the shower I am brilliant.

I feel so good about it, I start to sing. And wouldn't you know it, I sing very well in the shower. Professional quality, I believe. In fact, I am convinced that I might have a career on the Broadway stage if only I could do all my singing under a hot waterfall. Unfortunately, at the moment, the roles are probably limited, except perhaps for the lead in "Singin' in the Rain."

(I think I could tap-dance in the shower, too, if the floor wasn't so slick. I know I can do all sorts of Brando roles, including the "I-coulda-been-a-contender" speech.)

Anyway, while mulling life under a hot shower, I got the idea that other people probably feel just the way I do. I got the idea that all sorts of disagreements between people, all sorts of anger, would dissolve if negotiations were held in the shower.

I think, for example, that if the baseball owners got together with members of the players union in one of the showers at Yankee Stadium, the strike would be over long before the hot water ran out. I'm convinced of it. They've been meeting in the wrong room.

The thing is, it's hard to hold a grudge in the shower. Ask married couples who shower together and they will tell you. They may argue miserably going in, but after 15 minutes of steamy bubbly, it's honeymoon time coming out.

Yes, just today, as I was rubbing soap over my bald pate, I got to thinking that I like myself better in the shower. I even look better in the shower, or so I feel. There is no mirror in the shower and if there were, it would get all covered with steam.

I feel taller in the shower. Younger. Sort of debonair. I feel like Fred Astaire. "Heaven, I'm in heaven ..." I can do that!

Do you have a problem with me? Let's discuss it in my shower. I'm sure we can come to an agreement.

In the shower, I am mellow. You know, I think, maybe my editor really did have a point when he stepped on my previous column yesterday. He works too hard, the poor schnook.

It is quite likely, now that I think about it, that Einstein dreamed up his theory of relativity while reaching for his shampoo. In the shower, you don't need a blackboard with all those equations. The water makes complex problems dissolve and answers obvious. If I could organize the world, the U.N. would meet in a very large shower. Don't tell me there'd be a Middle East crisis with Jews and Arabs rubbing soap on each others' backs. (They'd probably laugh a lot, too. People look funnier in the shower.)

But, well, I can't organize the world. So probably nobody will take me seriously. So conflict will continue. And good ideas, along with good baritones, will be scarce. I don't care. I happen to know that showers do work.

For example, would you believe I didn't have an idea for this column until, in my frustration, I decided on a hot shower? And now here it is. The Pulitzer Prize people know where they can reach me.

March 4, 1995

PAWS AND REFLECT

I HAVE BEEN NEGLECTFUL of mentioning my cat, Hershey, and I think it bothers him. I have written about all the others in my family at one time or another. Hershey (yes, he's chocolate brown) has not rated a line.

Hershey is somewhere around 16 years of age, which for a cat is not the same as the "sweet 16" the rest of us enjoy. Arthritis has set in.

Hershey was adopted as a tot back in Massachusetts and although I am sure he was hoping for a life on Beacon Hill, he has not complained (much) about the hand life dealt him. For example, he has this heavy fur coat best suited for cold winters, not hot summers. Stuff like that.

Hershey has never been my cat, exactly. He was a gift for the kids. But the kids are all adults now and gone from the homestead. Hershey is still here and so am I. So we treat each other the way a couple of aging adults tend to do, with toleration, if not with an excess of benevolence. He needs his naps. So do I.

Anyway, I was feeling guilty the other day because, as Hershey moped by with nary a nod, I remembered that I hadn't put him in the column the way I had all the other Frymers. And while he hasn't done a helluva lot, or said a helluva lot, or even lived a helluva lot, he deserves better.

Whether he is my cat or not, I must admit that I have learned a few things from Hershey, things useful in my own life. So, to give him his due, I thought I'd mention them today:

———— ∞ ————

16 RULES OF LIFE, ACCORDING TO HERSHEY

1. You sleep better when your dish is full. (This is why I show up at the office every Monday no matter how I fantasize about running away to Tahiti.)

2. It is OK to kiss the hand that feeds you. (But stop short of fawning.)

3. Though a barking dog never bites, treat the threat in front of you as a possible exception. (In other words, don't put your trust in homespun homilies.)

4. If you can't be tough, be cute. (It works for me.)

5. The three most important things in life are a) food, b) sleep and c) sex. If you are neutered or a person over 50, it's a) food, b) sleep and c) regular bowel movements.

6. Take time to think things over, no matter how long it takes.

7. Everybody needs his or her own space. (Once you have found it, never let it go.)

8. If you are known to be friendly in the neighborhood, housewives will smile and call your name as you go by. (Old cats and old geezers like that.)

9. You can have more fun with a tennis ball than 300 channels of cable TV. (Even when the tennis ball has lost its luster, it comes with no commercials.)

10. If you're lucky enough to get stroked once in a while, don't forget to purr.

11. Learn to appreciate solitude. It's very restful.

12. Keep a clear perspective of all the alternatives available to you in life. When you discover that you have run out of alternatives, be loyal.

13. If you're a pussycat, don't try to bark. No one will believe you.

14. When you start feeling sorry for yourself, remember the homeless.

15. You only go around once in life. (Don't buy that rumor about nine lives, unless you believe in Shirley MacLaine.)

16. When the boss is paying for your food, don't pee on his carpet.

Well, OK, Hersh. Here's looking at you, kit.

April 6, 1995

OLD WHAT'S-HIS-NAME

Y WIFE WAS TELLING ME about a friend of ours. What's-his-name.

"You wouldn't believe what he looks like now."

"He?"

"What's-his-name."

"Oh."

"You remember. We went to see ... uh ... that musical together."

"What musical?"

"Oh ... what's-it-called? The one by the English guy. You know who."

"We went with what's-his-name?"

"Yes. And that girl. You remember ... the French one. Oh, what's-her-name?"

"What's-his-name went with what's-her-name to see what's-it-called?"

"We all went."

"When?"

"Not that long ago. A year or two ago. Maybe it was more. Three or four. In San Francisco. Maybe it was in San Jose. You know, you had that funny tie on with the thingamajig.

"The thingamajig?"

"The one you bought at … uh … what's-that-place?"

"What's-that-place?"

"You know, over at Valley Fair."

"I've never been to Valley Fair. You go to Valley Fair."

"Well, maybe … uh … what's-it-called … that-mall? You know by Sunnyvale?

"By Sunnyvale?"

"Maybe it's Cupertino. Oh, you know! The place with the Spanish motif."

"Spanish motif?"

"Don't pretend you don't understand. Hacienda something. With the fountain. Or maybe a pond. You said you liked it. Over by, maybe it's 280. Or Stevens Creek. You know — that place."

"Well, what about that place?"

"Where you got the funny tie that you wore when we went with … uh … what's-his-name and his girlfriend. Maybe she was Swedish."

"To see what's-it-called."

"You know! We went in his car. The uh … whaddyacall those cars? With that thing that sticks up in the back."

"An antenna?"

"No, I know an antenna. The metal thing that runs across. What do you call them? I think the girl was French. You thought she had a big nose. Or too many freckles or something."

"What girl?"

"The one he went with for five months or so. Maybe not that long. No, maybe that was another girl, the blond. He used to go with dozens of girls."

"He?"

"You know, what's-his-name."

"Oh, yeah. Well, what about him?"

"I saw him. That's what I'm saying!"

"Where?"

"Over at that ritzy restaurant downtown."

"What ritzy restaurant?"

"Oh, you know. With that strange name. Coq au something. We were going to go. Near that new place, that big coliseum place. Where you took Ben or Paul for hockey or basketball or something."

"The arena?"

"How come we never went to that restaurant? We were supposed to go."

"So you saw him there?"

"I think so. It looked like him."

"You're not sure?"

"I didn't get a good look."

"Too bad."

"But I think he saw me."

"But you don't know it was him."

"No. But if it was him, he must have seen it was me."

"He didn't say anything?"

"Of course not. He probably doesn't remember my name."

"Yeah. Old what's-his-name never remembered anything."

April 11, 1995

ON MOTHER'S DAY

I GUESS IT GOES WITHOUT SAYING that my first homage to Mom is that she made it possible for me to be here.

But in my case, that goes double. Mom not only gave me life, but she chose to do it in Canada, not pre-World War II Poland, and for that I am very grateful.

Since we're all honoring our mothers Sunday, I thought I might recall pre-war Poland and my mother's determination to leave it at a time that proved propitious.

Mom, the youngest of nine children in Pocanow, a tiny village in southeastern Poland, grew up very poor. She has told us all the stories, about how eggs were a special treat, available only at Passover. Since she remembers chickens running amiably through the town, I've wondered why eggs were so rare.

Maybe it was because my grandfather had a little store and all the eggs were sold. Or maybe Mom's memory — she's nearing 88 now — is unreliable.

Mom fell in love with the tailor up the street, just like in "Fiddler on the Roof." That tailor was David, who, according to Mom, was part of a family even poorer than her own. David apparently liked Pocanow and thought his tailoring had a future. Mom was not so sure.

She decided to visit an older sister who years earlier had moved to Canada. It was quite an adventure for Mom. On the way west, she stopped in Paris, and she has not stopped talking about the sights of that city to this very day.

When Mom got to Toronto, her eyes opened very wide. It was so very different from Pocanow. She could not believe the beauty of the place, the apparent wealth of its people, and the joy in having so much opportunity. When she went back to Pocanow she blurted all this to David.

"I want to move to Canada. Please, let us get married and move there."

David was happy to marry but he did not want to leave Pocanow. His family did not want him to leave. Mom pleaded with him, but to no avail.

The opposition to their leaving Pocanow grew louder. My grandfather, who was the town's most revered man, was angry. Mom was his youngest and favorite child. He did not wish to have her move half a world away. In Canada, he told her, there were few Jews, little heritage, an uncertain population. Pocanow was home, a civilized place where she was safe.

Nevertheless, my mom remained insistent. She told David that she would not marry him. She vowed she would leave without him. She may not have meant that, but David wasn't sure.

"What could a poor tailor do in a place like Canada?" he wailed. "Oh, wait till you see it," my mother urged him. "You can be rich there. Your children will be rich there."

Happily, David's fear was finally overwhelmed by my mother's eagerness. They were married in Pocanow with great joy and then, with some trepidation, amid family tears, left for Canada in the fall of 1932.

That was just months before Adolf Hitler became chancellor of nearby Germany. Hitler screamed venom against Jews, but there was no newspaper in Pocanow and the words were unheard. Anti-Semitism was common in those parts. Pocanow had always gotten through it.

I was born some years later in Toronto when the name Hitler was very well known and hated. My mother and father rarely talked of their parents, their brothers and sisters back in Poland. All apparently died in the camps.

David, my father, never did become rich, not even after we moved to the United States after World War II. But he, of course, never had reason to regret my mother's determination. As for me, I have been arguing with Mom all my life. She still gets her way most of the time. And I am very lucky for that.

Happy Mother's Day, Mom.

May 13, 1995

MY FATHER

THERE'S A PICTURE OF MY PARENTS on my dresser at home. It dates to the time of their marriage. They look strange, unfamiliar, a little dour. Why did people of their generation look so serious in their photos?

I sometimes study my father in that photo, his dark eyes staring straight ahead, his tight curly hair, a somber face that I cannot read. I realize that I never really knew my father. It isn't that he left home or abandoned us. He was always there. But he was apart, a tailor who seemingly never stopped sewing. He had a workshop in the basement of our home in Cleveland and he would be down there, it seemed, most of the time.

I guess we never really talked. Or if we did, I don't remember what we said.

My dad was old country. A little man, about 5-foot-4, he was uneducated. He read a Yiddish newspaper, which I couldn't read. He didn't take me to baseball games. He didn't know sports or movies. He didn't tell jokes. He worked.

In my childhood in Toronto, Canada, Mom and her friends — a lively bunch — might take my sister and me to the beach. Dad seldom came along.

Dad did have a temper. When it flared up, he would shout at Mom. And that would be upsetting, because I would always side with my mother and that would make Dad furious. He might swat me if he was really mad. Then he'd take refuge at his sewing table in the basement. Mom would assure me then that Dad loved us very much, but I didn't like him much at those times.

I remember finding a photo of Dad carrying me on his shoulders when I was about 3 or 4. When I first saw it, the photo surprised me because in it he looked just like everybody's father doing a Dad kind of thing.

Dad had his friends who dropped by often. With them, it seemed to me, he was more at home, more congenial. Looking back now, I realize that Dad just didn't know how to be a dad. He had grown up in poverty-stricken Poland, immigrated to Canada in the midst of the Depression and had thereafter struggled to provide for his family. That, to him, was what you did as a father. And the struggle was constant.

Kids like me were respectful. We were really little adults. We tutored our parents in the ways of the new world. I interpreted letters for my dad, helped him fill out forms. I taught him to drive when, at 50, he purchased his first car.

I think he was proud of me when I did well in school. But it was not the kind of phrase that would come from his lips.

Once, in a difficult, unemployed time for me, I visited my parents, bringing my deep depression with me. Dad saw the pain, but words were not his forte. He stared at me and said, "Don't worry so much." It wasn't much, but I grasped those words as a statement of support and caring. Such conversational scraps stay in my memory.

My father died at 74, some 15 years ago. I remember the last time I saw him. I sat at the foot of his hospital bed where he was suffering from cancer. He told me again that I worried too much.

I was flying back to California that night and I said I would be back, though I knew it was likely I would never see him again. I told him I loved him. I think he said he loved me, too. I kissed him on his rough, grizzled cheek. I can still feel it. I thought I heard him sob as he looked away.

I went to the elevator. I was numb. Go back, I thought. Try to talk. This is a last chance. But there was no way. We just didn't know how. I took the elevator down and left. Upset, I did not want to go back to the house. Instead, in my confusion, I went to a movie.

I returned to Cleveland three weeks later for Dad's funeral. It was on my birthday.

June 17, 1995

RIP VAN FRYMER

I'VE ALWAYS BEEN A MORNING PERSON. Barbara, on the other hand, has always been a night person.

When we were first married some 300 years ago, I'd often get to bed 15 minutes before her and be wide awake and making coffee when she arose.

Over the years, however, our divergence has been growing. I seem to get sleepy earlier and earlier, as if I am still on Eastern time 15 years after switching coasts. My eyelids droop at around 9 p.m. on many a night (when Seinfeld isn't on TV to keep me going.) Then long before the sunrise, long before any rooster has roused, I am awake and raring to go.

But Barb likes to read at night and on days when she can, she slumbers well into the morning. It is getting so that I think of my life as the early shift and hers as the late. The cuddling must take place between 1 and 3 a.m., unless I've got something on my mind when I will awake so early that I am not sure that I even went to bed.

These days I like to eat dinner at around 5 p.m. The evening news has for me become the late news and I only catch Jay Leno's show when I wake up especially early.

I seem to have a lot on my mind, but it isn't the stuff that used to be on my mind. I used to have the average concerns, some more troubling than others. Lately, I am dreaming about myself in discombobulated chronological terms.

Many a night I am a vastly different age in my dreams. I am back in the Army trying to convince a sergeant that it is all a mistake. I am usually 35 or so. Other times I am back in college worrying about an exam in a course I never attended. Then I am about 20.

When I awake, it takes me a few moments to re-establish my real age and then, of course, it shocks me. Where have I been for the last 25-30 years, I wonder. I feel like Rip Van Winkle.

I seem to be worrying more and more each night about less and less, a misplaced bill, a forgotten telephone number. I may soon panic over nothing.

On rising, I have to put myself back in order piece by piece. Maybe that's why I rise so early, to begin the process. But, actually, I like being awake very early. I can waste an hour over coffee and the newspaper and still be way ahead of the game. I can go through correspondence, pay bills, or just mull things over, all in an atmosphere of cool, quiet reflection.

Yes, I think so much better before dawn. I really wish Barb was awake to appreciate just how sharp I am at that hour. Unfortunately, when she is awake, I have already begun to slough off, and when she is at her sharpest, I can barely pry my eyes open to join in the conversation. I am sure she thinks I am no longer interested or able to converse, but I can, I can, if only we do it at 5 a.m.

At 5:30 or so, I am very witty. I tell Hershey, my cat, some hilarious stories, though, unfortunately, Hershey is not a laugher. He is a yawner. Unlike me, he never has wide-awake times of day.

I really should write this column at about 5:30 a.m. You would love it. But my editors don't get to work until long after I have begun to wear down and by the time I put the final paragraph on my column, I can barely keep my head above the keyboard. It must be catching because I notice that when my editor reads the column he, too, seems to get inordinately tired.

It helps, of course, if I take a nap now and then. Naps can be very refreshing. Right about now I could use a nap. Maybe, if you take a nap now and I take a nap now, we can get back to this discussion in a moment and really find the whole thing much more fascinating.

Yes. I am sure. Excuse me. Zzzzzzzzzzzzzzzzzzz.

Sept. 30, 1995

THE EFFORTLESS VACATION

BARBARA THINKS rigor mortis has set in. And, frankly, I'm worried about it, too. The thing is, I hate to do anything that I define loosely as "a hassle." I find that over the years, my naturally adventurous nature has run smack into my developing aversion to hassles. You can define hassles any way you want, but my rapid definition would be: any effort that appears more trouble than it is worth.

Years ago the category was slim. Most everything seemed worth a try or a trip. Now the category is overflowing. Sometimes going to the supermarket to get a loaf of bread seems a hassle. Who needs bread?

What brings this subject up is the imminent arrival of that full-fledged hassle of hassles: vacation. Barb, I know, looks forward to traveling around the world in a kayak. My own hassle-aversion scheme is simpler. Maybe going to a movie. Of course, I have to do better than that. I am willing to stop at a McDonald's on the way. Barb's compromise is to scrap the kayak, but maybe visit more than one planet.

I have been looking for some time for the perfect vacation. You know, the perfect hassle-free vacation. First, this is what I feel must be avoided:

1. Awakening at 3 a.m. to take a 5:30 a.m. flight out of San Francisco. No destination, no matter what delights await you

eventually, is worth that. And red-eye, overnight flights take a week or two to shake off, at which time I am back home.

2. Organized trips, full of schedules and buses. Especially with a bunch of strangers who love hassles.

3. Places with very hot food and very bad water.

4. Beaches totally covered by hotels, no matter how pretty the view.

5. Trips that involve two days of travel, one there and one back. The one back is interminable.

6. Places where the guide books tell you to wear your wallet taped to your chest under your shirt.

7. Places where there is more traffic than the traffic I am hoping to escape here.

8. Places where everyone looks as old as I am.

9. Places that are very hot, or very cold, or very wet, or very dry.

10. Places where one of the listed attractions is sitting by the pool.

11. Places where they sell T-shirts that say: "My mom and dad went to (fill in) and all I got was this lousy T-shirt." Actually, places that sell any kind of T-shirts.

12. Places with discos, casinos, street vendors, or where they hand out bargain coupons for helicopter flights.

13. Places where people who look like me sit on a beach semi-naked.

14. Places where I have to rent an uncomfortable car to drive unfamiliar streets, maybe on the wrong side of the road, and be insulted in a language I don't understand.

15. Places I can't afford, but because I have a "deal" I spend outrageously, only to sober up when I get home.

16. Places where I have a deal, only to find that everyone else has a much better deal.

17. Places where everyone tells me, "You should have seen this place five years ago."

18. Places where everybody else is on vacation; sometimes even the waiters.

19. Any place that is all-you-can-eat or all-you-can-drink. I regrettably try to get my money's worth.

20. Any place in the middle of the high season. That brings on my low season.

Well, all this is only a part of my list. I could go on but I hate writing lists. You know why.

Nov. 28, 1995

MY DAUGHTER
THE BARTENDER

My DAUGHTER HAS FOUND A JOB as a bartender. That's after four years of a top-grade college, a degree in sociology, 10 years of dance classes and auspicious debuts in numerous productions. I'm delighted. I hear that bartenders make pretty good money, at least as compared to dancers. And it is useful work. There are probably as many people who find bartenders useful as those who find dancers and sociologists useful.

I have a nephew who earned a law degree and, given his wit and wisdom, we all expected him to be another Clarence Darrow. Now he fronts for the dregs of society as a criminal defense attorney. Mostly, he gets muggers off. There's a big market for that.

Another nephew who wanted to be a pop singing star now works as a telephone hit man for a credit card company. After his mother bragged for years about his beautiful voice, he now uses it to scare the living daylights out of credit scofflaws.

And down in Los Angeles, my good cousin, the fledgling screenwriter, cleans swimming pools for a living. Everybody in L.A. writes scripts, of course, but a good pool cleaner can clean up.

Yes, it's a tough job market out there. We are turning out lots of brilliant graduates these days and then turning them into cab drivers, pizza deliverers and sandwich makers. Apparently we don't really need so many brilliant graduates and we do need cabs and pizzas. That's how the economy works.

That doesn't mean that young people have to give up their original goals. It means that the path to glory can be pot-holed. Sometimes the pot-hole gobbles you up and you never get out. But that depends a lot on determination.

Having interviewed thousands of winners over the years, I have learned that failure is normal, that the road to success usually depends less on college degrees than on a merger of luck and endurance.

And something else. If you want to be a dancer, it helps if you can't really do anything else. If you can do something else, eventually it will become crystal clear to any would-be dancer that you should do something else.

Often the most successful artists, actors, writers and whatever are people who simply lacked the skill to achieve an alternative. If you are a dancer but also have skill as an accountant, it's damned sure you are going to become an accountant. I think people like, say, Woody Allen, became successful because on the whole they were occupationally disadvantaged. Could you see Woody working in the business world?

I wanted to be a songwriter when I was a young dreamer. I wrote about 1,000 songs a year, all of which are still in a big box in my garage. But it's hard to get a job as a songwriter.

I did get a job as an assistant editor for something called PR Newswire. I did a lot of assisting and little editing. Most of my assisting involved running for coffee, which I wasn't good at and eventually got fired. But I then had "editor" on my resume and when it appeared to me the world no longer wanted songs — at least mine — I turned to newspapers for sustenance.

That didn't turn out too badly, though I still think the world missed hearing a vast medley of Murry Frymer hits. Actually I still sing my songs in the shower, where they sound damned good.

As for all the young under-employed dancers, lawyers, singers and screenwriters, just remember your own tune and keep singing it. You may well have to change paths someday somewhere, but not till that last note has left your starving throat. In the meantime, mixing drinks isn't half bad.

Dec. 26, 1995

HERSHEY'S BIG MOVE

Hershey, our aging brown cat, has taken up residence in the garage. We put him there because he kept throwing up on our new wall-to-wall carpet.

This morning I went into the garage to feed him. He looked at me with wide yellow eyes. He was upset. "Yeah, I know," I said. "It's cold out here."

"Tell me about it," he said. "I've got chapped whiskers."

"Well, we spent a fortune on that carpet. It's Berber, you know."

"I didn't tell you to get such a light color. That color shows everything."

"Especially fur balls," I said. "Hershey, old cat, you are starting to be something of a problem. We're trying to be nice."

"You call this garage nice? Have you ever slept out here? This is winter. And I hear funny noises up in those rafters."

"Well, if we have a mouse, catch it. That's what cats are supposed to do."

"Not this cat. Do you know how old I am? I mean in cat years. I'm like 100. I'm another George Burns. Does George Burns catch mice?"

"Does George Burns throw up fur balls on the carpet?"

"OK, let's let bygones be bygones. When do I move back inside?"

'We're not sure if you will, Hersh."

"What? You're not serious, are you? Stop pussyfooting around!"

"Can you swear that you won't throw up again? Or that you won't spread fleas around the house? Or that you'll stop shedding over the new carpet?"

"Put a litter basket somewhere!"

"I said 'shedding.' Hershey, you are a mess. You're making the house a mess."

"I'm a cat. An old cat. At least you don't have to take me for walks."

"Well, we're thinking our relationship over. Right now we feel better with you in the garage."

"How come there's no window in here? What am I supposed to look at all day?"

"I thought you slept all day."

"How do you sleep in these temperatures? I really need some sleep. I could also use some warm oatmeal. This place is the pits."

"You'll get used to it."

"Yeah, and maybe you'll get used to my poop on the car hood."

"Pets better learn their place. Right now, this is your place."

"Ah, please. Listen to me purr. I'm a good cat. I'm a famous cat. What would all your readers feel?"

"Sympathetic."

'To you or me?"

"It depends on how they feel about fur balls on the carpet.

Anyway, I've brought you some real pieces of chicken here. Right off my own dish. I'm treating you pretty well."

"Wait till the kids hear about this. Call them and tell them 'Hershey is in the garage.' Tell them you saw me shiver. Tell them I was attacked by a mouse."

"I've got to go to work now. Have a nice day."

"Well, don't go writing about me in your dumb column. This is embarrassing. Find something else to write about."

"No problem. I've got lots of things to write about. I'll see you tonight."

"Yeah? Well, watch out for your backside."

I left Hershey not altogether happy with his situation. I wasn't too happy myself. Hershey and I really have a lot in common, except for his long hair. We are both getting older. We both sleep a lot. We both have bad stomachs.

It makes me think. What if I wind up in the garage someday? What if I get put out here because I mess up the house?

What a thought. Who would do such a thing? I better remember to buy some flowers for Barb.

Feb. 3, 1996

MURRY IN THE DOG HOUSE

By Hershey Frymer, Cat columnist

M Y MASTER IS UNABLE TO WRITE his column today. He is sitting alone staring out the window and looking kind of pale. So I have decided to help the poor jerk out. (By the way, I use the term "master" just to make him feel a little better. Cats, as most everybody knows, have no masters. Let me get that purrfectly straight right up front. Excuse the cat joke – I can't help it; I've never written a column before.)

The hundreds of calls and e-mail messages started hitting the fan before 7 a.m. Saturday, about the time Ol' Mur's misbegotten column about sticking me in the garage hit the front lawns. Ol' Mur had said he had taken action because of my fur balls on his new Berber carpet. I guess he thought he'd get a few laughs. Hsss! From the garage, I could hear he wasn't getting any. "These people have no sense of humor," he whined. (Columnists whine for a living.)

Of course, the lack of sense was all his, and he learned that as the morning wore on. Mercury News readers are exceedingly kind. To cats! Columnists are at best tolerated when they don't make trouble, but Ol' Mur (my pet name for him) had clearly crossed the line.

Some of the callers provided information on how to rid

me of fur balls. Others had advice on how to keep that precious overvalued carpet clean. But some said – in unrepeatable language – that he should move himself – and the carpet, too – into the garage and return me to my rightful place inside the house.

By Saturday afternoon, he stopped checking his messages, pulled the shades, and began coming into the garage every 10 minutes, hoping I would say something to bail him out. Naturally, I looked the other way. (I hate it when humans look especially frail.)

When my sweetheart Carrie (his daughter who, believe me, is much too good to him) called from New York to say she had heard from a friend who read the column what he had done to me, Ol' Mur buckled. He brought me back in and opened a can of turkey giblets, which is my favorite.

I gave him a few purrs to buck his spirits, though he still looked kind of vacant as he scratched his flea bites. I walked around the house to get my bearings again before settling into a bedroom closet where I have a collection of fur sheddings I am saving.

Unfortunately, in Ol' Mur's haste to bring me back in, he didn't allow me to lick off my paws. I had just stepped into the litter box and, well, my toilet habits are absolutely immaculate – but it takes an old cat a little time to clean up!

Anyway, it wasn't long before Ol' Mur noticed the new dark brown path I had made on the new carpet as I hurried through all the rooms. He got a look on his face that, well, I'd describe it, but I don't think I've seen that look on humans before. I thought his fur-ball look was bad, but this was kind of really hideous and I had to shut my eyes and pretend to be asleep.

Listen, I feel for the old simpleminded guy. Before any of

you start throwing fur balls at his car, remember, he's been pretty good to me for 17 years. I should tell you about the time I broke my leg, but space is running out.

Anyway, the features editor here, who has two cats of her own, says she might get me my own column and maybe eliminate his. I have some great stories of my youth in Massachusetts. (You wouldn't believe the dogs there and how fast I was!) It's more interesting than the stuff Ol' Mur writes, and I work cheap, a little Meow Mix, which publisher Ol' Jay finds very reasonable.

So this whole thing has turned out OK. Except for Ol' Mur. You know, I'm really beginning to feel for the guy. Of course, he had to learn his place.

Feb. 6, 1996

COUNT YOUR GESUNDHEITS

BARB WAS COUGHING AWAY at the kitchen sink when I said, "Gesundheit!" Amid the coughs, she rasped, "You say 'gesundheit' when a person sneezes, not when she coughs." And I said: "Why? 'Gesundheit' means good health. Why just worry about a sneeze?"

And she said: "You can't say it for everything. You say it for sneezes." And I said: "You should say it for everything. How come a sneeze rates so much concern and a cough nothing?"

And she said: "Well, it just sounds weird to hear somebody say 'Gesundheit' when you cough." And I said: "I think we should say 'gesundheit' when a person belches, too. It means you've got a bad stomach. That's a health problem."

And she said: "So if I burp now, you're gonna say, 'Gesundheit?'" And I said: "Or 'God bless you.'"

And she said: "I hope nobody hears you." And I said: "And when somebody passes gas. You should not just yell out, 'Who f———?' You should say 'God bless you.'"

And she said: "You're insane. Who, in his embarrassment, at a time like that, would want to hear somebody like you say, 'God bless you'?" And I said: "It shows my concern."

And she said: "It shows your rotten manners." And I said: "My rotten manners? I didn't let out that big bazoom."

And she said: "Whoever did doesn't need a 'gesundheit'

from you." And I said: "It couldn't hurt."

And she said: "Believe me, it couldn't help. You let it pass."

And I said: "You let the gas pass. You let the gas pass without so much as a 'God-bless'?"

And she said: "And the cough and the burp, too." And I said: "But you've got to say it on the sneeze?"

And she said: "As far as I am concerned, you can skip the sneeze, too." And I said: "Never say it? Never say 'gesundheit?' Never say 'God bless you?' OK. Go tell it to the Pope. He says, 'God bless you' all the time. To millions of people."

And she said: "Yes, but not when they sneeze." And I said: "When they cough? When they pass gas? Could you imagine a million people passing gas?"

And she said: "That's awful. God will get you for this." And I said: "I'm only concerned for your health."

And she said: "Your mind doesn't work right." And I said: "I'm only being thoughtful. People say 'gesundheit' automatically. Why? What is it about a sneeze that makes people say 'gesundheit?' What are they worried about? And why do they worry in German? Why don't they worry in Spanish? Or Arabic? Or English!"

And she said: "Go away. Go somewhere." And I said: "And if they worry about a sneeze, they should worry about a cough, too. And those other things."

And she said: "OK. It's your bedtime, go think about it in bed." And I said: "I will. I'm going to sleep. Don't wake me."

And she said: "Unless you snore like you always snore. Believe me, if you snore tonight, you know what's gonna happen? You're going to hear something in your ear. A big loud 'GESUNDHEIT!'

And I said: "So you do care! God bless you, Barb."

Feb. 29, 1996

SAY SOMETHING, DAD

Every so often I come across an interview with some very famous person who, inevitably, credits his or her success to some fatherly advice.

"My father once told me," the story goes, "do unto others as you would have others do unto you." Or something like that. And I think, that's great. The old man at the dinner table once said something pithy and the kid remembered and grew up to be chairman of the board.

Then I stop to contemplate: How come I've never said anything like that? What advice have I left my kids? If my kid gets to be president, is he or she going to say: "As my father once told me, look both ways before you cross the street"? Yes, I have said that, but somehow I don't imagine my kids will remember to give me credit for that memorable remark.

I get depressed. Here I've had 20-some years raising three fine children, and I don't think I've ever said anything memorable to them. Does "Clean up your room before you go out!" leave a lasting impression? Or did "You are not going to wear that bathing suit to the beach!" influence my daughter to embark on a career as a world-famous dancer?

I don't get it. I had all those years to say things that they would take with them every day of their lives.

"Ask not what your country can do for you, ask what you

can do for your country!" would have been good. Oh, that would have been very good! But JFK beat me to it and now look how well his kids turned out.

Or I might have said one day, as the kids were pummeling each other, "If you can keep your head when those about you are losing theirs and blaming it on you," or however old Rudyard put it to his kid. They remember things like that, if only I had gotten them to shut up once in a while and listen. I think I once told Paul: "Wise up!" But it's not the sort of thing he would tell an interviewer.

Sometimes even questionable rules get remembered. Willy Loman (in "Death of a Salesman") told his son: "Biff, you've got to be well-liked." I say that's questionable because it leaves out any mention of character and perseverance. So Willy Loman got criticized by his son. But I've always felt that Willy wasn't totally wrong, haven't you?

Anyway, I've been trying very hard, while my kids still call once in a while, to come up with something memorable. The trouble is the most memorable lines have already been taken.

When the kids were youngsters playing soccer, I told them: "It isn't whether you win or lose, but how you play the game." Ben looked up at me as I lifted him from three feet of mud in which he was lying and said: "I don't want to play this dumb game. I want to play my video." So I dropped him. He won't tell the interviewer about it, I hope.

Anyway, when Paul called last week about his limited resources, I said: "A penny saved is a penny earned." He asked to talk to his mom, who is sending a check. He will probably remember that longer than my memorable words.

Still, I keep a Bartlett's by the phone, in case I can come up with something in the nick of time. I've got a lot of good ones. For example, "To be or not to be, that is the question."

Of course, one of the kids is going to have to ask me, "Dad, what is the question?"

Or maybe, in a moment of thoughtful repose, one will wonder, "Dad, what is it we have to fear?" I will respond: "Carrie, the only thing we have to fear is fear itself."

Then, 20 years hence, when Time magazine is interviewing her, she will remember and tell the reporter. I hope they spell my name right.

April 9, 1996

MAKING A LIVING

I HAPPENED TO STOP at one of the stock brokerage offices
the other day, and I noticed a lot of older men sitting there
watching the big ticker. You know the tickers I mean. The
stock prices travel by from one side of the wall to the other,
greeted by stares from the (mostly older) men in front. They
are getting richer or poorer as they watch, but if it's poorer,
wait a minute.

It seemed to me to be a strange way to pass a day. But I
suppose getting richer or getting poorer does have some interest. A lot of people pass the day with even less novelty.

An awful lot of people lately seem to be passing their days
staring at screens, like I'm doing right now. Words go by or
numbers go by. It's sort of interesting, but then, sitting in front
of a screen isn't the life lots of us might have picked out.

My father passed most of his life sewing. He was a tailor
and he'd sit with his old sewing machine or a needle and
thread for hours on end, for days, for weeks, for most of his
life. I used to wonder what he thought about as he sat there.
Did he find it reflective, thoughtful, or was he numb most of
the time? I do know he was often very proud of his work, so I
guess he was one of the lucky ones.

My mother, on the other hand, cooked all day. She cooked
breakfast, cleaned the dishes, cooked lunch, cleaned the dishes,

cooked dinner. That might seem terrible to some, but I think she loved it and now, as she ages, misses it. My mother didn't have a paying job till the kids were grown. She worked at sewing alterations, which was OK because of all the women friends she made and chatted with.

Most people spend most of their days on the job. We don't think of it as life, but "making a living." There are people who make a living calling other people on the telephone, asking them to try something or buy something. These people get hung up on all the time. Sometimes the people they call are really perturbed and bang the receiver. Not me. I really feel sad for people who call me at dinner hour suggesting I buy something, but I don't buy anything. I figure it's a strange way for someone to spend their days.

There are people who do oil changes all day long. They turn a screw or something and all the dirty black oil from the crankcase comes out and then they put clean oil in, and that's their day. It may seem simple but problems arise to make for variety.

My postal carrier spends her days going from house to house dropping off the junk mail. It's not a bad day considering you get exercise and fresh air and there are all sorts of people like me who peer from the windows, waiting.

Dentists drill teeth all day and deal with very nervous people. Prostitutes have sex all day long with strangers they don't care about. But there's lots of personal contact.

I mention all this because I find it fascinating what people do all day. Most people really don't realize that what they are doing hour after hour day after day is their life. Most people think they are doing all these things for a while 'til their real life begins.

I used to think that, until I woke up one morning and realized how old I was and how much time I had spent doing what I was doing. It was my life, not just my day.

My father's life was sewing. My mother's life was cooking. My life has been newspapering. In between, we all had kids, raised them and sent them on their way to have a life.

When I retire I may go down to the brokerage and watch that ticker all day, talk with the other guys and tell stories. It's probably not a bad life.

April 11, 1996

WATCH THAT WASTE LINE

'WASTE NOT, WANT NOT." To you, maybe, just another one of those aphorisms. To you, maybe. To me it is a lifestyle. Hell, I think it's an illness.

I've got a definite need within my soul to make things last. To not throw away that which has maybe another five minutes of use to it. The bar of soap I use in the shower gets down to a see-through shard as I attempt to rub some lather out of it. I squeeze my toothpaste tube to flatness and beyond.

I know it is insane, but someone breathed, "Make it last" into my ear when I was an infant, and so help me, I can't shake it. Throwing something away that I could use a bit longer is one of the 10 deadly sins to me. Am I just cheap? No, I have totally different standards where Barb and kids are concerned. But I just can't think that way myself.

Each time we are about to donate some bundles of clothing to one charity or another, I examine my donation most carefully. So what if the shirt collar is just a tiny bit frayed? It's still a nice shirt. I'll wear it weekends.

Needless to say, people snicker behind my back, or so I fear. But it isn't my contempt for fashion. I am thrifty. I am forlorn. But have compassion, please. I can't help it. Yes, I believe in cleaning my plate, unless the food is making me positively ill. Maybe even then. I think it was my mother who first introduced me to the concern that "people are starving in Europe." Someone would appreciate the scrap I was about to discard. So I ate it. I was chubby as a toddler.

My mother still uses an ancient kitchen knife she brought from "the old country." It has a moonshape cutout on the blade from its decades of use. It is still kept sharp.

I own a living room chair that I think is unsittable. For most people, not me. The foam rubber has been worn to where the chair resembles a toilet. But I like to sit and read there. The light comes from a lamp that visitors think is an antique, but it was new and modern when I bought it.

I bring this up because a couple of weeks ago I did something unusual for me. I bought a new car.

That was the easy part. It was trading in my ancient Subaru that was hard. In fact, to get it ready to trade in, I had it washed and waxed and it looked real good. As I drove my new car away, I tried hard to avert my head from the lonely lot where my trusty old Subie sat. It was painful.

The next morning I awoke not to the joy of my new car but to the agony of not seeing my old Subaru in the driveway. I had traded it in with a full tank of gas, too. Talk about waste. I am, of course, pleased by how much better my new car drives. But Subie had, I believe, another good year to give.

Every once in a while I feel sad about all the great new things I could buy if I could get over my obsessive frugality. Why should I not experience lots of new cars, at least to the point of affordability? I could get a closetful of new clothes and impress everybody. I could trade in my superworn sneakers for some Air Jordans. I could live!

Nah. You don't just toss out perfectly good sneakers. You don't flush a usable bar of soap just because it is nearly invisible.

I live in fear that one day, while carousing around town in my nifty new sedan, I will run across my old Subaru, now being driven by a scruffy youngster with a lead foot. Aha, I will think. Subie did have a few good miles left.

Barb, of course, is well aware of my affliction. She has given up trying to change me. But I tell her at least she can be assured that I will never divorce her. What, and waste a perfectly good wife?

May 7, 1996

MARRIAGE:
THE SATURDAY NIGHT
SOLUTION

I WAS LISTENING TO A MARRIAGE expert on KQED the other night. Actually, I think she was a divorce expert, which of course, is a better gig because it's in far greater demand. Anyway, this woman was telling the interviewer why, despite soaring divorce rates, some marriages do manage to last.

Barb at the time was sitting in my recliner reading and not paying any attention to me. When she reads, which is a lot, she does not let me turn on the TV. It's not like she's reading "War and Peace," mind you, but that's another column.

Anyway, in the silence of that family room, I had nothing to do but listen to Barb turn pages. So I flicked on the radio, softly, and I listened to this female expert discuss the wonders of successful marriages.

I gather that this woman is an expert because she has managed to be married for umpteen years. But then so have I, and I don't need her to tell me the secret of successful marriages. What is it? Two words. Saturday Night!

Saturday Night is what drives people to get married and what keeps them married against all odds. It is the yardstick by which, from the age of 5 on, we judge ourselves. It works like this: If you have a date for Saturday Night, you are a winner, a man to be admired, a woman who is desired. However, if you are alone on Saturday Night, you are a midget, a hapless soul whose worth is clearly on the ebb. You are nobody, nothing, nada.

I don't know where this dictum was first ordained. I think it probably came down with the Ten Commandments – "Thou Shalt Not Be Alone On Saturday Night." But Moses, in his chagrin, chopped it off the list because the poor schmo never had a date on Saturday Night. (It's hard to lead your people out of bondage and still get dates.)

Anyway, when I was growing up (as opposed to the current growing down), I had this rule burned into my brain. In my teens, whenever Thursday came, I was already in a sweat. Inevitably, some buddy would ask, sort of matter-of-factly, "What are you doing Saturday night?" And I would cringe. "Oh, I've got plans," I would say. Plans to hide under the bed.

Mom would leave me alone all week long. But on Saturday night, if I was sulking in the living room, she would ask, "Nothing to do on Saturday night?"

And so, of course, I found something to do. I got married. And, with memories of Saturday Night, I have clung to this marriage arrangement come what may.

Marriage is the foolproof solution to Saturday Night. Even if you have, as usual, nothing to do on Saturday Night. You're married! You don't have to have anything to do on Saturday Night.

My point is that it is the inbred fear of Saturday Night that cements so many marriages and keeps them devoted. It is the secret of a successful marriage. It is what makes marriage last.

Divorce, of course, is what happens when one of the married couple actually finds something to do on Saturday Night.

But that's another column.

It is wonderful to have the Saturday Night dilemma solved. Since I married Barb I have been a happy man. I think she is happy, too, though once in a while she wearies of reading and insists I take her to a movie on Saturday Night. OK, fine, you do that for love. And yes, we are deliriously happy. We have plans for Saturday Night.

I was surprised that the KQED expert never brought up Saturday Night in her discussion. But I figured she was just too embarrassed to reveal the simple truth. The interview, pointedly, was on Saturday Night. She had something to do.

June 11, 1996

BEAUTY AND THE BEACH

THE LOVE SONG OF J. MURRY FRYMER, or shall I carry a copy of my newspaper rolled:

It's another Sunday at the beach in the charming little town of Capitola, sometimes called Capitola-by-the-Sea, to distinguish it, perhaps, from Capitola-by-the-Desert. And here we are at Zelda's-by-the-Beach. We are the mature pale couple in the midst of tiny bathing suits worn by tanned young hunks and perfectly formed lovelies.

"I don't think anybody here is over 25," Barb says, adjusting the sweat shirt tied around her waist. We carry sweat shirts in case a breeze comes up. No breeze today. It's hot and incredibly bright. I am the one wearing a Yale cap, a polo shirt and long tan pants. I look perfectly attired for a horse show.

I peruse the scenery. At the next table there are two sassy lasses of the sophomore persuasion. They are wearing skimpy little swimsuits and sipping from glasses of green liquid, filled with ice and topped by slices of lemon. One of the young ladies really should never have come out of the water, given the inadequacy of her covering. But, then, with the possibility of shrinkage, she probably doesn't go near the water.

As luck would have it, at the table next to these two, are two handsome young men, tanned, bright-eyed, topped with

— what I am quick to notice — are mounds and mounds of excessively thick, curly hair.

"I used to look like that," I tell Barb. "Really?" she says with a scoff. "Not since I've known you."

The adjoining young men are making funny little remarks to the young ladies. I assume they are funny because the women are giggling constantly. I smile. I used to be funny, too, though I never was rewarded with that much giggle.

The waitress keeps asking us — the mom and pops of her rounds — if we are all right. If the food is all right. If the drink is all right. I think she is worried about us. I do see one grizzled older man sitting alone at a table. He has his knee bandaged, is smoking a cigarette, has a big radio boom box on the table. Except for the grizzle, a local affectation, he appears even more out of place than we. Smoking? In these environs, that's like cutting down a redwood tree. I think he feels the vibes and leaves.

The crowd is effervescent, boisterous. So much sun, so much skin and so little time. The young men next to us are saying wondrously inane things to the appreciative young ladies. It seems such an effort. The foursome has joined at one table now and ordered two big pitchers of green liquid with lemons.

And then behind us another young man begins to sing. He has a guitar hooked up to a blaring sound system and his repertory is country music. His style is borrowed. He sings and groans, tells musical tales and gets mild applause. Barb and I would have preferred something from Bach or even Rodgers and Hart. But I don't think the chattering young crowd is here for the music.

Many more young ladies arrive, barely contained in their little two-piece suits. Male eyes, including mine, follow them around. Mine eyes have seen the glory but now the heat is strictly sun.

The incessant young man behind us is singing something about American pie, the foursome at the next table has become positively giddy and young waitresses keep coming over and asking if everything is all right. Everything is all right. Except everybody is far too young here. I know I was once this young, but in my case it only lasted a weekend.

Actually, things are really nicer for me now. I don't have to say silly things to Barb to keep her interested. She has a shrimp-and-avocado salad for that.

June 25, 1996

I MEAN,
YOU KNOW WHAT I MEAN?

I AM TRYING MIGHTILY TO GIVE UP saying "quite frankly." Apparently, I say it all the time. I say it so much I don't really hear it. But it must be very upsetting. Barb says that she is thinking quite frankly of leaving home.

Actually, I also say "actually" a lot. I don't know why, actually.

Of course, I am not the only one who has a pet expression that seems to tumble out with every breath. There's a buddy of mine who is always saying "as a matter of fact." As a matter of fact, that's quite like "quite frankly," actually. Lots of pet expressions seem to have "fact" in the phrase. I know people who say "point of fact" to make a point of fact every time they speak.

"To tell you the truth" is a lot like that, too. The speaker says something like, "I was thinking of having chicken for lunch, but to tell you the truth I really prefer beef today."

Weird, huh? I mean, is that bit about thinking of having chicken a lie? Maybe people who say "to tell you the truth" all the time are letting you know that they don't tell the truth except at those moments when they are willing to tell the truth, which they then tell you.

But these are mild afflictions. The one that drives me wild

is "You know what I mean?" You know what I mean? My father-in-law used to say, "You know what I mean?" about six times in every sentence. Not only did I have to listen to that, but he expected an answer. Yes, most people who say, "You know what I mean?" expect you to play along. For example:

"I'm at this store and this guy looks at me funny, you know what I mean?" "Yeah."

"And he starts looking at me up and down, you know what I mean?" "Yeah."

"But he doesn't say anything, you know what I mean?" "Yeah."

"Huh?" "Yeah."

"Huh?" "Yeah."

"You know what I mean?" "Yeah."

Quite frankly, this kind of repartee can drive you out of your mind in minutes, you know what I mean? Nevertheless there appears to be no way to stop it. If you say, "I don't know what you mean," the speaker will only repeat it all with new emphasis. What you really want to say is, "I don't give a damn what you mean, so cut it out!" Of course, I never said that to my father-in-law.

Then there are those people who have to say "like," like, you know, every minute. In this case I have no idea what "like" means. It's, like, meaningless. That's the way with such phraseology. Most of it is meaningless. People walk around muttering, "What are you gonna do?" every few minutes, but don't want you to tell them what you think they should do.

I do think that if we could eliminate these little pat expressions, human conversation could probably be cut in half, which wouldn't save the redwoods, but would probably aid against noise pollution. In fact (another expression), I think most people couldn't really talk at all without their little expressions to get them through sentences.

I want to say to them all: "Gimme a break. Like, really, get a life, you know what I mean?"

"Like, wow, man, I really need to hear that."

But what're ya gonna do? Huh? You know what I mean?

Yeah, that's what I'd like to say, but, quite frankly, I haven't got the nerve, actually. And, I'm sure, nobody would know what I mean.

Aug. 22, 1996

HAPPY NEW YEAR, GOD

A CONVERSATION WITH GOD at New Year's (the Jewish one):

"Happy New Year, God."

"You, too, Murry."

"I'm glad I was able to get this interview."

"I don't give many, son. But your column needs help."

"I'm sure it will. Help, I mean. With your influence, I mean."

"Don't count on it. Some miracles are hard even for me."

"God, I've been wanting to ask you something. This seems a good time. I don't go to services as much as I should. Does that upset you? What I want to ask is, do you favor those of us who are religious?"

"You mean, do the religious win points with me?"

"Something like that."

"That's a very good question, Murry. Sometimes they do; sometimes they don't."

"Sort of a riddle, eh, God?"

"No riddle. Some of the devout are among my best creations. They know my heart and seek to do good. Others of the devout are just, well, devout."

"Interesting. I'm glad to hear it. I mean that you note the

difference."

"You think I'm a dummy? Easily swayed by form without function? It's one thing to say the prayers. It's another to be a mensch."

"Yes. Ha-ha. You know the language."

"I know all languages. By the way, your English could use work."

"Yes. But tell me: Why are religious people getting into so much conflict? And so often in your name? Why do Catholics kill Protestants and vice versa? Why do Jews and Arabs hate each other? Why are Muslims and Catholics at war in Bosnia?"

"More good questions. You are not wasting this interview. OK, this is something that breaks my heart. That people should kill in the name of faith. I think they think I want them to. No. Look through all the religions. It's love, not war, I preach."

"How come we get it wrong?"

"My question, exactly. How come you get it wrong?"

"Well, what should we do?"

"Get it right. You know that Golden Rule? Simple thing. It works."

"Anything else?"

"Yes. Call your mother once in a while."

"God, what is going to happen to us here on Earth? I mean with all this hatred and stuff."

"Oh, don't get depressed. Look around. There's a lot of good people down there. Follow their example. They know my heart."

"Thank you for that. Does the human race have a long future? A good future?"

'Another good question. Murry, I'll have to start reading your column. Listen, don't worry about the future. I'm into the present. Be honorable. Be kind. Show character. Get with it."

"Is that your New Year's commandment?"

"It's my every year's wish. Never changes."

"And if we follow your wishes, will that bring everlasting joy?"

"Don't make deals. I'm not into deals. That's the problem with some of you people. Do good for its own sake. And don't worry about it."

"But what will become of us? Will the religious go to heaven? Will the faithless go to hell?"

"This is why I don't give interviews. People are too nervous. Look, go home, hug your wife and children. Give strangers the benefit of the doubt. Practice charity. I'm here. It'll be OK."

" 'It'll be OK!' Oh, thank you, God."

"No problem."

"Maybe we could do this again?"

"Sure, we will. But, Murry, next time don't call me. I'll call you."

Aug. 14, 1996

NATTERING IN THE OBITS

I GUESS IT'S WHEN YOU REACH AGE 50 or so you discover a page in the newspaper you didn't know was there. It's the obituaries, a collection of personal stories about lives - sometimes notable - just concluded. Oh, it sounds grim, but it is really not so depressing as Page One, where all the murders and plane crashes and other daily horrors are recorded.

The reason for the obituary is death, but these are stories about life and how we live it, for good or ill. It is a page of biographies, summations, tributes and, as a way of score-keeping, numbers. Almost all obituaries and their headlines have numbers in them - the age of the deceased. That's a critical part of the score-keeping.

And the easy part. How well or how poorly the deceased lived takes more information than the writer of the obituary usually has on hand, often more than any of us may know. So the newspaper prints the age of the deceased up front, because that, at least, is salient fact.

I said that interest in this page grows as you reach 50 or so. At that point you begin to compare your own age to the ages in the obits. Are you older, younger? You can't read the obit page without being very aware of where you stand on the mortality charts. The older you are, the more likely the obits will include a onetime friend or acquaintance. Or all those celebrities who were part of your world and are, to your amazement, leaving it.

It's curious what in our lives is remembered. Sometimes for the more famous it's a single action or phrase. For example, when Spiro Agnew died, virtually every obituary referred to the Agnew speech wherein he called the press "those nattering nabobs of negativism."

Agnew probably didn't write that himself. Reports are that it was speech writer (now columnist) William Safire. But the remark stuck to Agnew more than anything else for which he was known, including years of corruption. I wonder if Agnew realized when he spoke of us nabobs that that was the way he would be forever remembered. Would he, perhaps, have preferred another memorial?

Most of us have no such quick handles. We are not "Wrong Way Corrigan (or Riegels)." Our lives have no singular event or phrase that is memorable. We are, instead, a collection of many events, successes and failures, misplaced hopes and occasional dreams-come-true. Obituaries are a tough story to tell.

So we get the score-keeping. How many wives? How many kids? How many homes, degrees, from which college? What were our jobs? And, finally, of course, how did we die? Even some of this can be fascinating. I shout over to Barb: "Hey, did you know that so-and-so had five wives?" And she makes her own summation: "He must have been a' louse to live with." It doesn't say so in the obit, but all those scores give us clues.

Still, few obits really get to the nitty-gritty. I'd like to know the day on which the deceased was happiest and why? And before his heart stopped, was there a day on which it was broken? Whom did the deceased love the most and did she marry him? And what did the deceased have to do to earn so much money and did it please or bother him?

Sometimes newspapers interview famous men and women prior to their deaths. The interviewee, I would guess, is careful in what he says. Why leave a lousy last impression?

I wonder if the famous would like to read the obit before it runs. They certainly can't read it, or correct it, after. I don't know that I would want to reveal anything painful or foolish to an obituary writer. I think I would mention that I once shared some laughs with Lucille Ball and that she thought I was very funny. Stuff like that. Yeah, put that right up front.

Oct. 1, 1996

UP TO MY ASH IN MUD

Calistoga

Ok, MY NAME IS MUD. I never really expected to get into that big vat of hot slime here at Dr. Wilkinson's Hot Springs. It was all Barb's idea; she is a bit the flaky Californian in this regard. But me? I'm a rational Eastern transplant. I joke about hot tubs.

The woman behind the desk looked at me with some distress. "You're not going to do it?" she asked with what seemed like disbelief. "Really?"

It was as if she recognized someone who needed the mud. I was put on the defensive. What had she seen? I hemmed and hawed and haw-hawed. She said: "You really should! You'll feel wonderful!"

Barb jumped on this spiel. "Do it," she urged. "You'll feel wonderful!" Then the woman found my Achilles' heel. "There is a special price if you both do it!" she said. The magic words. I will do anything if the price is special!

And so I found myself disrobing. I wondered if I should keep my shorts on. Salvadore, the attendant, wondered if I wanted stinky, muddy underpants. Then he led me to the vat room, where there were three caskets filled about four feet high with black, chunky gunk. Volcanic ash in hot mineral water, he said. Whose ash was it? I joked.

Salvadore told me to jump in. The mud was deep and hot, bubbling on top. Crazy. Pigs did this kind of thing - not smart people like me. OK. OK. I put a foot in. Yu-u-uck! It was hot. It stank.

"Lie down," Salvadore said. Somehow I managed to lie down on top of the stuff. I was sort of floating. Salvadore came back and pushed me down into it. Deep into it. "Yeeeow!" I said. "Hot."

He was unimpressed. "You gotta take off your glasses," he said. Holy sheep dip, I thought. He's not going to push my head under, is he?

"You want mud on the face?" "Mud on the face?" I panicked. "Special mud," he said and began smearing me with what felt like face cream. Thank god, I muttered. I was not being buried.

Salvadore looked down at me. "How you feel?" he smiled, as if everyone always said, "Great." I didn't feel great. I wondered how many had been in this vat before me. The mud is supposedly sterilized after each customer, but, well, when you are lying in the black, messy stuff you have to wonder. Was I in poopie peril?

Mud baths are sold by Wilkinson as a "stress stopper." How come I was stressed? But then, after a while, I did relax. I looked at the head in the vat next to me. Its eyes were shut. Maybe it was dead.

I listened to the music. It was something fluty, spiritual. I would have preferred a Broadway show.

I shut my eyes, dug my fingers deeper in the ooze. It felt nice and warm. Think happy thoughts, I reflected. I sighed. I think happier thoughts in front of a fireplace or a prime rib dinner. But what the hell. This must be doing me a lot of good.

After 10 minutes of the mud, Salvadore pulled me out. "The works" then included a whirlpool bath, a long, sweaty steam bath, a ice-pack-on-the-head "blanket wrap" and a half-hour massage from Charlie, who looked a lot more like Santa Claus than the muscular masseur I expected.

Afterward, I met a glowing, pink-cheeked Barb back at the room. "How was it?" she gleamed. "It was good for me," I murmured seductively. "Was it good for you, too?"

Nov. 26, 1996

I SHOULD'VE...

THE YEAR IS LEAVIN'. Which leaves me grievin'.

I should've gotten started writing my great American novel as I had promised myself last January, and the January before that. I have a nice stack of paper next to the computer at home, neat and clean and unused.

I should've had that long talk with the kids telling them how proud I am of all the things they've accomplished, but mostly of what good people I think they are. But everybody was always running off here and there and somehow I never made time.

I should've watched less sports on TV. I can never remember the game five minutes after it's over and yet I get all caught up in watching, day after day, week after week.

I should've watched less TV, period. What a terrible waste of time that tube is. How much of 1996 did I blow transfixed like a dummy in front of my 21-inch screen?

In lieu of my record, I should've made fewer comments to Barb about how much time she "wastes" watching a daily soap opera.

I should've written fewer political columns. I am terribly biased toward my side and that only encourages the calls and letters of people terribly biased toward their side.

I should've taken myself less seriously. God knows everybody else did.

I should've stopped and smelled those roses I planted in the back yard. Those yellow beauties failed to get the attention they deserved and it probably made them sad.

I should've sent some notes to writers on this paper and elsewhere who show great talent at what they do. I hunger for such applause myself, then forget to offer it to others as much as I should.

I should've laughed more.

I should've shown more outrage at all the phonies and rip-off artists who prey on the public and too often get away with it because we weary of protest.

I should've watched my cholesterol more. But, alas, there were times when a pizza and only a pizza was the answer to a lingering funk.

I should've bought Intel and IBM stock early in the year.

I should've done that curtain-call dance at the conclusion of "Anything Goes," my stage debut with the American Musical Theater of San Jose. I was afraid of making a fool of myself and demurred.

I should've shown less fear of making a fool of myself.

I should've bought flowers for Barb once in a while for no reason at all.

I should've lost 10 pounds.

I should've flossed more.

I should've read some of those books I keep planning to read but, succumbing to the TV, don't.

I should've thought of Christopher Reeve every time I felt sorry for myself. And every time I loudly lamented the ignominy of some human beings, I should have remembered the incredible courage of others who daily overcome terrible burdens.

I should've slept less.

I should've forgotten about O.J. Simpson.

I should've spent more time with our family photo albums. Nothing brings greater perspective than an hour or so with those pictures of my life.

I should've eaten my broccoli.

I should've cried more. Why do I keep pretending I am not moved when I am?

I should've listened more. I insist on solving other people's problems when they merely want them heard and acknowledged.

I should've paid more attention to 1996 and not let it slip away as it did. 1997 will be different. I will begin my great American novel. I have the paper all in place next to my computer.

Dec. 21, 1996

MURRY-MURRY
FRYMER-FRYMER

I AM RUSHING THIS COLUMN into print as fast as I can, but, drat, you've probably already read a whole slew of witty opinions about cloning. And, I suppose, they are all pretty much the same, stuff about replacement body parts and the like. You might say that when a juicy topic like this comes along, the columns are quickly cloned.

However, now that we know that cloning of humans has become truly possible, we should approach the topic with the utmost seriousness.

First off, let's drop the ethics debate. As we all know, when we make decisions on what we want and don't want, ethics only get in the way until somebody who sells stock in the What-We-Want Company comes along to enrich us. Let's assume we are already there.

Do I really want a clone? Yes. I want a clone for all sorts of dandy reasons and I'm not even counting body parts. (Yet.)

My clone, of course, will be a younger version of me. Ah, how I'd like a younger version of me! My clone will have silky, curly hair, piled high on the left. Ah! My clone will walk with a jaunty air instead of a slouch. What's not to like?

Beyond appearance, my clone will be fresh. His brain will

be uncluttered with all the generations of regret and rejection that have encumbered mine. He will be cheerfully optimistic and might well achieve what I no longer try. It would be the Second Coming of Murry, only I will be around to teach him all the things that the first Murry screwed up. He will be a Smarter Murry with Hair. The possibilities are limitless.

I think it will be fascinating to watch Murry-Murry Frymer-Frymer (my clone) go through life. (When we have clones, we will probably all name them like that so as to indicate they are repeat versions. If my clone had a clone, it would be Murry-Murry-Murry Frymer-Frymer-Frymer. What a fabulous byline.)

But I don't think I will let my clone go into journalism. For one thing, this business is floundering, on the ropes, probably because of columns like this. I want Murry-Murry to work for Microsoft, maybe buddy around with Bill Gates or Bill-Bill Gates-Gates. Or, who knows, he could become a star of show business, something I neglected to do despite the definite possibilities. Look, Murry-Murry would have my DNA!

Then there is the question of romance. When I think back at all my faltering steps, this is one area that will require careful tutelage. Will my clone fulfill my greatest fantasies, or marry a clone of the woman I married? (I should point out for the sake of domestic tranquillity that the two choices are not mutually exclusive.)

The whole thing fills me with great wonder. My clone Murry-Murry, he'll be tall and as tough as a tree, will Murry-Murry. Like a tree he'll grow …

Wait a minute, I am confusing a clone with a kid. I already have three kids. And they have never learned from my mistakes, no matter how carefully I taught. My clone will probably pay no attention to me, either.

And wouldn't that be a kick in the pants! Imagine having a clone that talks back. I would be having arguments with myself.

Imagine a clone that sits around all day wasting his time and has high cholesterol. I'd have to watch that klutz do all the dumb things I have done and not change a thing.

No, when you get right down to it, those replaceable body parts might well be the only good thing about clones. And Murry–Murry, the jerk, would probably be less than generous about his. I know his type.

So go ahead, send in the clones. I'll pass on mine.

Feb. 25. 1997

HERSHEY'S
UNFINISHED SYMPHONY

By Hershey Frymer, Cat Columnist

WHAT I NEED RIGHT NOW is a seeing-eye dog. I can't see very much at all and I'm walking into walls. Ol' Mur has to pick me up and take me to my food dish or the litter box. What an embarrassing catastrophe!

I keep rubbing my eyes, and it's taken off some of the fur on my forehead. Now I guess I look like Ol' Mur. I hope Barb can tell us apart.

Well, it's like what Barb's dad used to say: "Don't get old!" Barb remembers that when she talks about me. She has to talk loud. I don't hear well, either.

My stomach is giving me fits. But I can handle it. I am not infirm. I am still my lovable self, and I purr twice as loud to prove it. Ol' Mur is getting old, too, you know. Lately he's forgetful. He leaves sheets of his Mercury News on the floor all over the house. Very messy. Whenever I throw up, I am careful to avoid hitting one of the newspaper sheets. I respect this paper. I am a columnist here.

Now for the good news. All the kids came home for the Passover dinner last month. What a feast! And I didn't even know I was Jewish. The kids look different now, all grown up. I remember them when they were tiny. We were all tiny together. I got a lot of cuddling, and then they left to go wherever they live. So it's back to mostly Ol' Mur and me now.

He lies around the house, watching TV and sleeping. I lie mostly on a box in Ben's bedroom. Yeah, Ol' Mur and me have more and more in common. Though my column is more popular than his ...

Note: The following is written by Murry Frymer:

I AM SORRY TO REPORT that Hershey didn't finish his column. He died May 21 at the Humane Society of Santa Clara County. Hershey was just short of his 19th birthday, which Humane Society people said was pretty old for a cat, though for an old cat, he was still pretty.

Hershey was born on a farm near Boston, Mass., in August 1978. Easily the pick of his litter, with his mink-like dark brown fur (which gave me the inspiration for his name), he was adopted by an excited Frymer family and, a year later, accompanied us to San Jose. We were all homesick for Boston for a while, but Hershey managed to turn our tract house into a family home in no time. He guarded it incessantly, on the front lawn or the back fence. Any criminal cats in the neighborhood kept their distance and the Frymers felt safe.

And, of course, he was always the center of attention, the one Frymer who never was out of sorts, who always greeted our returns with excitement, who made us better people than we would have been without him.

I must admit that I was very ignorant about cats when he joined us. I'd never had a pet. I thought they were just bother and mess and expense. Hershey taught me different. He taught me values about loyalty and love and endurance. We bonded. He needed me and that was nice. But I came to need him, too, and that was a surprise.

Hershey was pained by untreatable maladies and, finally, it seemed best to give him rest. But it was not easy. At the Humane Society's little euthanasia room, Barb and I wept silently as we held him and watched the end. The two society people treated him with kindness. The woman said: "We don't want him to think it's his fault."

Hershey had been frightened earlier, squirming to escape, but now he was calm, brave. One paw was shaved, a needle inserted in a vein and then he just slumped, the tip of his tongue visible. He was gone. We were left alone, the three of us, with a printed prayer. The end had come quickly, and Hershey appeared not to suffer.

I cannot say the same for Barb and me, who, tear-stained, drove silently back to the home that he had warmed for so many years and which seemed very empty when we got there.

May 29, 1997

MY OLD HOUSE

IT'S ONLY A HOUSE, an old house, but it was my old house. Mom moved out last week to an "assisted care" facility just down the road. Mom will celebrate her 90th birthday on July 4th, a regular Yankee Doodle Dandy. I was in town to help and, of course, take one last, long look at the place where the family had lived since the late '50s. Mom lived there alone for the last 16 years.

It's a nice house, or so I think. Clearly, it would never be featured in House & Garden, although I remember when we moved in we considered it the ultimate in classy living. There is a paneled basement, which Dad turned into his workshop. In the master bedroom, there is a built-in desk with book shelves. But no master bath or Jacuzzi.

There is an enclosed "sun room" which extends out from the house into a nice yard, lush green right now with a big oak tree for shade. The oak has grown to massive proportions, still doing its job. I wandered around the house a couple of days ago, and I must admit, it doesn't look classy now. Some of the furniture remains, though many of the chairs need assistance, maybe a home for aged furniture.

The dining room set isn't half-bad. The glass-fronted hutch contains Mom's prized collection of decorative cups and saucers and the wine glasses I sent from Venice so very long ago. The table, kept protected during those boisterous family meals of yesteryear, has been polished regularly. I look around and remember the holidays when Dad presided at the head of the table and the room was packed with family, including seven rambunctious grandkids running noisily this way and that 'til Mom carried in a roast chicken and begged everyone to please sit down and eat.

If I wanted to, I could almost hear the voices. I could certainly smell the food. And the pleasure beaming from Mom's and Dad's faces is clearly ingrained in my memory.

Ah, the kitchen through the swinging door. It was Mom's command post where the marvelous high-cholesterol dishes were designed, developed and produced in daylong efforts that spared nothing fattening. No one had ever heard of cholesterol then. We knew only our abundant appetites.

The rooms are still decorated with family pictures. There is my framed, tinted high school graduation photo on the old black-and-white Dumont TV set. The set hasn't worked in years, but the wood console with doors was too nice to discard.

I look at my photo. Ugh. I can't believe I once looked like that and still managed to find a lovely lass to marry. Thank you, God.

There are lots of photographs around, some still on table displays to be collected later. My wedding photo. My sister's wedding photo. The kids as babies, as infants, as toddlers, as teens. I wander through the rooms, past boxes of ancient letters. My letters, my sister's letters, old birthday and holiday cards, even old gas bills.

I find a box of business cards I once had printed for Dad when I was urging him to open his own tailor shop. He never did. In the basement there are still tailors' chalk and thousands of buttons and bits of cloth and various supplies for the sewing machine.

An old radio that was a bank gift. Pictures on the wall that look like paint-by-the-numbers art. Everywhere there is "stuff." Mom, in her later years, saved everything, especially anything I sent. The drawers teem with a variety of items, all with stories, stories that overload my memories. I decide to leave.

It's only a house. I am stupidly sentimental about houses, and old cars, and old pieces of chalk. Mom has a nice new place. She doesn't have to cook. The staff serves delicious low-fat meals.

I leave the light on in the kitchen, lock the door and drive away. Next time I'm in town, a new family will be there, new photos, and no tailors' chalk in the basement.

June 19, 1997

VITAMIN P

I AM GOING TO LIVE FOREVER. That's because of vitamins. I take them all and I glow.

It all started for me with Linus Pauling who, you may remember, told the world the glowing advantages of vitamin C. I used to be a scoffer at such things and I scoffed at Pauling back then. He not only recommended taking vitamin C, he recommended taking it in doses that looked like sacks of flour.

He said he hadn't had a cold in 20 years. He said he was going to live forever and, as I remember, he almost did. I figured that was good enough for me, so I began gulping the stuff. I, too, did not get a cold, though I did spend a lot of time in the restroom, getting no rest.

But that was just a start. Certainly you've heard about vitamin E. I did and I got some. Actually, I got lots. And then beta carotene. It was either that or eating carrots with the frequency of Bugs Bunny.

Last week I stopped at Trader Joe's for the latest hot pill. Vitamin B — super B — with folic acid! That, too, is great for the heart. And I'm for that. I guess the health people finally began to get wind of me. General Nutrition wanted a picture for their walls. I'd try anything. I went around singing: "You've gotta have heart ... miles and miles and miles of heart ..."

A couple of weeks ago I received information about a new

miracle therapy, only this time I didn't have to go to Trader Joe's for a bottle. This boon to health was already … uh, around. It's called urine therapy. According to the news, it's "a natural alternative that works." And therein followed "an amazing untold story."

Well, I think you're already wise as to why the story was untold. According to writer Martha M. Christy in Nexus Magazine, "There is an extraordinary natural healing substance, produced by our own bodies, that modern medical science has proven to be one of the most powerful natural medicines known to man. Unlike many other natural medical therapies, this method requires no monetary investment or doctor's intervention and can be easily accessed and used at any time."

The author goes on to say that "extensive medical research" has found that this therapy "can produce often astounding healing, even when all other therapies have failed." I must admit that at this point I was both enthralled and disgusted. I am a health shopper and a bargain hunter and this product seems to fit both bills. But I have sought to live a life of good taste and this somehow didn't fit in.

Who in the world would try this? Well, according to the article, very well researched it seems, there is none other than Henry Kissinger. Kissinger is reputedly a … well, there is no other way to put this … urine drinker. I used to gag at his foreign policy, but I never dreamed of this.

I cannot prove any of this myself, of course, and I know I may be considered guilty of yellow journalism. I am just telling you what I am reading from supposedly reputable sources and I am doing it as primly as possible. Proponents of this therapy well understand the resistance it might have and suggest that for those so bothered, you could start with a dribble in your morning juice. They also say lots of other disgusting things, including using the liquid for eye and ear drops.

Health is of vital concern in all our lives, of course, but I must say that I am not willing to follow everywhere the mavens lead. For one thing, I think this kind of therapy will definitely get in the way of my accustomed good-night kiss. I don't want to wind up tremendously healthy and ignominiously alone at the same time. Maybe Kissinger doesn't care or Richard Nixon didn't.

But I don't want to dismiss the health field entirely, either. I really don't get as many colds as I used to. Folic acid sounds like a winner, and maybe it will help with my follicles, too. But you have to draw the line somewhere.

I will drink no wine before its time. Or afterward, either.

Aug. 21, 1997

ON THE FRINGE

SOME PEOPLE LIVE IN ABJECT FEAR of going to the dentist. Me, I live in terror of going to the barber.

It's not that I need a haircut very often. I am seasonal. I need a trim in spring, summer, autumn and winter. And I'm thinking of eliminating winter, when I need to keep my fringe for warmth.

When I enter a barber shop I become intensely aware that I am in foreign territory, among people who look drastically different from me. All the chairs are filled with Elvis Presley types whose massive curls are being adjusted, arranged and perfumed. I feel like I used to in my dating days, when I inadvertently wandered into a lesbian bar. What the heck am I doing here!

Well, I do still have a little cuttable hair — yes, I do — though, regrettably, it is not ideally placed. It grows on the back of my neck and if unattended it goes south from there. When it appears ready to reach the middle of my back, I know I have to go to the barber.

Given these limitations, I have tried to get my wife to snip it off, but then she becomes very emotional, realizing her husband is Big Dome and she could have married some hirsute glamour boy and instead she has to wear sunglasses in the house because every time I pass under an overhead light I blind her.

Look, I live with it. Bald men make bald jokes, but not when we are alone with only a mirror. Then we are the bald joke.

And when I enter a barber shop, well, not only is the place totally mirrored, but I am aware that all the hairy, vain men there stare in horror. I am a living example of a worst-case scenario. I sense fear on the stricken faces around me.

So I sit down and sigh.

"How would you like it cut?" the barber asks.

"Like that guy over there," I say pointing at Elvis Presley.

The barber laughs, sort of. Presley laughs, sort of. I don't laugh.

"You want just a trim?" I am asked.

"Whatever," I say.

"Whatever you want," he says.

"Whatever I got," I say.

So he goes to work. Snip snip. Five seconds later he's done.

"You want me to trim your moustache?" he asks.

"Sure," I say, terribly shy about leaving the barber chair so soon after getting into it. "And get the ears. And the nose." And any other outlaw hair that skipped out on my head and got planted elsewhere.

Why is it, I have wondered, that men who can't grow hair on their heads seem able to grow the stuff virtually everywhere else? I even have hair on my knees. My beard needs twice-a-day shaving. My eyebrows are wild and woolly, a veritable jungle. But my head? The Sahara.

Another problem I have with barbershops is the price. It used to bug me to pay five bucks for a haircut. Five bucks for five hairs, I used to complain. But barbers are "hair stylists" now and haircuts have gone up to $11 or $12 or $13. And a nice little tip is required to round out the transaction. Usually the barber is embarrassed when I tip, but he takes it.

I feel that barbers ought to charge by the hair or by the minute. I could get away paying about a buck. Including tip.

I sigh again and prepare to leave. I toss the Playboy magazine, which I barely had a chance to open, back on the stack. The barber, trying to pretend that he actually worked on me, takes a hand mirror and puts it up in front of my face, adding insult to injury. "Yeah," I say. "Perfect."

The sweeper, who usually has to clean up around the chairs for other customers, stares at the floor around my chair as if he is going blind. And then I go home. Where it gets worse.

All men who have had their hair cut like to hear from observers at home. "Nice haircut," is an appreciated compliment. The last time I heard that was when I was 12. Now my wife might say, "Say, did you get your hair cut?"

But, of course, I only hear that when my back is turned.

Oct. 30, 1997

MR. AND MRS. MOSES

I T'S HARD TO GET RESPECT AT HOME. Rodney Danger-
field is not alone. A column or a talk may go over well with
the public, but at home, well, the standards are much higher.

Which made me wonder if the great men of history suffered the same ignominy in their own kitchens. For example,
let's say, Moses. Now there was a great man. He certainly earns
applause in the Bible. But at home?

———— ∞ ————

MOSES' WIFE: "Where were you? Your dinner is getting cold.
Why don't you let me know if you are late?"

MOSES: "You wouldn't believe the day I had. You will be very
impressed."

"Impressed schmessed. Where were you?"

"I was summoned to the top of Mount Sinai."

"Summoned? By who?"

"Wait 'til you hear. By God. By God himself."

"Uh-huh."

"Did you hear? God summoned me."

"Listen, you want anything with your fish? Some
horseradish?"

"You're not impressed? He summoned me to give me the Ten Commandments."

"He gave you Ten Commandments? Like he couldn't find some big-deal guy who would know what to do with Ten Commandments?"

"He happens to think I am a big-deal guy. He is very impressed with me."

"Sure."

"Yes. He chose me to give the commandments to the Tribe of Israel."

"Where is Israel?"

"It's across the Sinai Desert. He wants me to lead the Hebrew people to the land of Israel. What do you think of that!"

"I think that you ran across some con man at the Pharaoh's and you got taken again. What did you pay for those rocks?"

"What pay! Those tablets in the living room are God's word!!"

"Moses, I love you, but you are a shmegeggi. You have a problem with your self-esteem. You have to pretend you're somebody or you met somebody. Now it's God."

"What are you talking about? What is self-esteem? I tell you I saw G-O-D today."

"And I saw Elvis Presley. Go eat."

"I am going to lead our people to Israel!"

"They are going to follow you? The way you read maps? Remember on our vacation we were supposed to go to the Nile and you wound up at the Red Sea!"

"Hey, that's another thing! When the Egyptians chase us, God is going to part the Red Sea! So Jews get through the water and Egyptians drown."

"Hoo boy, this Pharaoh's crook probably sells time shares. You're such a schmo."

"Well, a lot you know."

"OK, so what does God look like? Tell me that."

"He looks like a burning bush."

"Pardon me?"

"He looks like a burning bush. Only the bush is not consumed. It's quite a trick."

"So I know, you really stopped at that Egyptian bar, Faisel's, on the way home. And where did you get those filthy stones? You gotta get them out of the living room!"

"Are you kidding? Are you kidding? Those are the Ten Commandments. Those are the most important words ever written!"

"You mean you can get something for them? From two big rocks?"

"They were written for us! God said we are the Chosen People!"

"Moses, how do you think this stuff up? Maybe you could make movies!"

"Movies will be made about ME! Just wait till you see Israel!"

"And how are we going to get there? Tell me that!"

"We are going to walk."

"And the Egyptians are going to chase us?"

"Right."

"And you will be the leader?"

"Absolutely. God chose me."

"My mother was right. She told me to marry Shepsl. He's a

doctor now. Listen, you go to Israel and send me a postcard. And take those two big rocks with you. The cleaning lady is coming tomorrow."

Nov. 4, 1997

ORGASMS KEEP YOU YOUNG

I've been away mulling the meaning of life, and while I was mulling I read that there was a new study comparing men's sex rates with their life spans. I held my breath on this one. I don't know how men would react to the news that the more sex you have, the shorter your life would be.

So I was more or less pleased that the study worked out the other way. The more sex men have, according to a group of British doctors, the longer they live.

Good news or not, most men probably shrugged off the story. For one thing, we have all known this or assumed this or guessed this. Sexual activity is one of life's more pleasant interludes, and pleasantness obviously helps men endure. (And endure pleasantly.) Like, for example, a good glass of wine. Studies in recent months have indicated that a glass a day does wonders for the heart. If you haven't got wine, scotch helps.

Anyway, back to sex. The study, reported in the British Medical Journal, says that "men who have more orgasms seem to live longer." The participants in this study were Welsh men in the town of Caerphilly (pronounced care-fill-ee, and yes, when I read that I wondered if the study was a put-on, but apparently not).

Anyway, back to sex. Having regular intercourse reduces the risk of death by about half, according to the analysis, or as

Dr. George Davey-Smith puts it nicely: "Sexual activity seems to have a protective effect on men's health."

OK, there are all sorts of ways this study might be skewed. For example, the sexual partners. Do men who date or marry sexy women live longer than other men? You have to see the connection. Then there are other health matters. Do men who marry women who suffer frequent nocturnal headaches live shorter lives? If so, I can anticipate desperate scenes in many a bedroom, where she says, "Not tonight, dear, I have a headache" and he says, "Headache shmedache, my life depends on this!"

And if that is the case, would a woman who denies a man be legally culpable if he dies? You could charge manslaughter. Johnnie Cochran could play the "sex card." (Say, did you ever notice that manslaughter is the same spelling as man's laughter?)

Anyway, back to sex. If these recent studies are to be believed, it is important for men to at least try a glass a wine and sex once a day (in no particular order) and see what happens. In fact, I imagine there will be further studies on this matter in the United States. To understand sex, we have to do more than watch Wales.

If we did have a sexual study in the United States, I imagine that getting volunteers would be no major problem. Unless, of course, you were placed in the placebo group. Those unfortunate souls would get no wine, either, before or after its time. (I don't know about this group's death rate, but its attrition rate would undoubtedly be high.)

Anyway, back to sex. There is a lot more of this we need to know. I, for one, need to know just where women stand, or don't stand, in this matter. I would like to ask women: Was it good for you, too? It would be absolutely awful to learn that sex benefits only men, which would turn romance into charity, about which of course much has been written in a lot of bad novels.

And what about a cigarette after sex? Does this defeat the treat? And is red wine better than white wine? And if she says no, does it help to whine? And if sex twice a week halved the death rate of men who had sex once a month, as the study says, how about sex twice a day? Yes, how about it?

There is so much that we need to know. I think that Dr. Davey-Smith should keep studying. And so should the rest of us. Really, it's a matter of life and death.

Dec. 30, 1997

IDEAS, IDEALISM AND I

There is another journalism.

Some years back, the editor of the Levittown Tribune was a young man in his mid-20s. It wasn't his newspaper — the owner lived in a grand home on the wealthy North Shore of New York's Long Island. The owner had 15 weeklies. He never came to Levittown.

The pay was bad. The hours were endless. But the young man thought of himself as a "journalist." Idealism dripped from every pore. He liked seeing his name under the editorials as "editor."

The young man lived in a small apartment in Manhattan, 90 minutes away on the Long Island Expressway. Single, he needed a more socially exciting environment than suburbia. But in short order the young man purchased a folding cot from the Woolworth's store across the street and slept on it in the office on various nights of the week, especially the night when all the news copy had to be sent to the printer.

The office, upstairs of a cleaning establishment on Hempstead Turnpike, was small, just a desk and files and a little counter on which the postmen dropped the voluminous mail. There was no receptionist, though a local photographer helped out when he could. He needed plenty of notice. He was no paparazzi.

The only other person involved in the enterprise was an artist who drew caricatures on a freelance basis and supplied editorial cartoons to the editor's specifications once a week.

Levittown, the first massive housing tract in the nation, had been developed by William Levitt in the 1950s — 17,000 homes on potato fields, selling first to World War II veterans for $6,500. The widespread community of little boxy houses became something of a joke to the big city press, but to the young editor of the weekly Tribune, this was a huge, vital community, filled with critical news that the residents needed.

And that took 20 hours a day and it took tremendous energy and it led to daily exhaustion. The young man attended lots of meetings. The school board on Wednesday nights rambled on past midnight and often led to a night on the cot in the Tribune office. Housing boards, sewer boards and cultural affairs also depended on his coverage.

There were constant squabbles. One of the biggest, a story that made it into the city dailies, was an effort by the conservative bloc on the school board to ban some well-known works of literature from the English department curriculum. The young man was in the middle of it, covering the story, writing the editorials and ducking the flak that came at him from all sides. It was tiring. It was exciting.

Oh, and there were the big football games at Levittown Memorial High that had to be covered, the wedding notices and the obituaries that needed delicate handling, the people who won various prizes, the speeches when someone notable came to town. It was all attended, written, designed (hopefully with a photo) and then gobbled up each Friday by the community.

There was the day that John F. Kennedy died. A shocked,

tearful Levittown told its story in the Tribune. That issue sold out quickly.

Readers loved the Tribune and sometimes didn't. The letters column was filled with praise and complaints. But the young man grew quite important in the community, attending all major affairs, dining with all the key players. He wrote about how people were redesigning their Levitt homes, about the people who arrived from elsewhere and the old-timers who left. The young man believed he was the cement that held the town together. Some residents thought so, too.

One election day, the young man wrote an editorial supporting the Democratic candidate for local office, a fine woman, he thought, with some worthwhile programs. On the day that appeared in print, the young man was fired. The owner on the North Shore supported the other candidate.

The young man, stunned, folded his cot and drove back to Manhattan.

Now, decades later, he still delights at a letter from a one-time reader or an offspring who recounts some story, some squabble, that the young man wrote about a long time ago in the Tribune.

Sept. 9, 1997

WHAT'S IN A NAME?

WOULD YOU BELIEVE IT? I have a cold. It is worse than a cold. I feel really icky. My eyes and nose are runny and my stomach is sort of the same. You definitely do not want to get too close to this page. Oh, did I mention I have a headache, too? And my hands are clammy.

I should be home in bed, but I am nothing if not courageous. I am the Cal Ripken of columnists. I think I have gone generations without a sick day, and that may be my only claim to fame. Indeed, many a day my column has been sick, but never me.

Anyway, Barb really doesn't like me around when I am sick. There is nothing like sneezing and coughing to test a marriage. No wonder Mother Teresa never married. Also there is the matter of sharing with readers all sorts of vital, insightful, inspirational … uh, whatever. For example, today I am writing about a new list of most-popular names. Michael tops the male list. Followed by Christopher, Anthony, Kevin and Daniel.

I can't remember when Murry was on the list. I think my parents picked my name from the 10 least popular. It was right up there with Leo.

Murry is usually a joke name. Neil Simon often has a "Murr(a)y" character in his plays who is a certifiable idiot. (How can a 'Neil' cast aspersions?)

Anyway, we were talking about the names of saints the other day, what with Mother Teresa very likely to join that elite group, and it was pointed out that while there already is a St. Teresa (Santa Teresa locally), there has never been a St. Murry.

I said that lots of Murrys are saintly but they are too timid to point it out. What this world needs is a Pope Murry I who would not only be saintly but would also give the world a good laugh every time his name was mentioned. And that would do the world a lot of good. I can't remember a pope you could smile at, much less feel superior to.

I once interviewed the playwright Murray Schisgal and the name Murray came up. He shrugged and said all Murr(a)ys are alike. They all have freckles on their backs, are bald and tend to put up with a lot of guff. But, said Schisgal, they have a boiling point, and someday the world is going to be blown up by a Murr(a)y. I don't know what happened to Schisgal, but I definitely don't open unsolicited packages from Murr(a)ys.

I note most of the names on the most-popular male list are biblical. And that may be the problem. I am not a biblical scholar, but I do not recall a Murry in either the Old or New Testament. And that's good. If there had been a Murry at the Last Supper, he would have been the waiter. Who would drop the dishes. And Jesus would say: "Oh God, it's Murry!"

Does any of this have a point? Of course, only I am feeling way too lousy today to remember what it is. And I'm getting low on Kleenex. And everyone in the vicinity of my desk has moved away. I carry on.

Did you know that Kevin, the fourth most popular male name, is very unpopular with men but very popular with women, who apparently have the upper hand in naming their kids? I get that information from the American Names Society Journal. Also, I note that Robert was the most popular male name in the '40s and early '50s, but has disappeared from the top 10 entirely. The same with John, a biggie in the '20s.

Also, parents have all sorts of fancy spellings of girls' names but tend to spell boys' names without any flourishes. Except for the fact that my name lacks an "a," which is a long story that I don't feel like telling with runny eyes.

And speaking of the American Names Society Journal (was I?), I think that's a very unsexy name for a magazine. I like sexy names. The most popular female name is Ashley, and that makes me think of characters out of racy novels. Again, you'll never find a Murry in a racy novel.

But enough about me. Barb said I could never write a column feeling as miserable as I do, and once again I have proved her wrong. And, yes, Hall of Fame, I remain the Cal Ripken of columnists.

Sept. 23, 1997

ALWAYS A MOM

I FIRST LEFT HOME as an 18-year-old, heading for college. Mom, with tears in her eyes, stuffed a couple of $20 bills in my hand. I resisted, but Mom was never one to take "no" for an answer. And back then I could use the money. Which, I guess, was the original reason behind what was to become a ritual. After every visit, Mom, with tears in her eyes, pressed bills into my hand.

Of course, it became a bit odd as I moved into my 30s and 40s, a married man with children of my own. Now, Mom had a few dollars for each of the kids, too. And, insistently, for me.

I fought against my farewell gift vociferously and at great length. It did no good. Mom would never allow me to go without that money, stuffed into my hand at the door. It was to pay for the air fare, or "get something for the children" or "take your wife to dinner."

Mom, who didn't write checks, always kept a little cash in the house for exactly these occasions. It was never a great deal of money, but I knew it was a lot to my mother. The bills were always old, rumpled paper that appeared to have been kept in a roll for many months.

"Mom," I would yell when I reached my 30s. "I have lots of money. I don't need this. You need this money more than I do. I don't want it."

But there was no way she would let me give it back. Once, in anger, I threw the money on a table, but Mom, chagrined, retrieved it, stuffing it back into my hand. "Take it, take it," she said. "It cost you a lot to come here."

Yes, it was sort of perturbing to think that Mom felt I needed the money. But that wasn't really the reason for the gift. It was, in her mind, protective. She had grown up in poverty, first in Eastern Europe, then through the Depression years in Canada. When she could no longer stuff food into my belly, she stuffed bills into my hand.

I visited Mom again just a few days ago. Suffering from senile dementia, she lives now in an "assisted-living" home in a Cleveland suburb. It is an attractive place, but even so, the elderly residents seem grim and helpless.

Mom is especially frail now, a few months from her 91st birthday. She recently suffered a hairline fracture to her spine, limiting her further. She says she didn't fall, but she may not remember it or may wish to deny her vulnerability. She insists her pain is arthritis.

After a few days together, it was time for me once again to say farewell. At which point Mom suddenly remembered she needed her purse. I protested as she hunted it madly, hobbling, panicky, around the room. She found it by her bed and sighed in relief. Inside were a few rolled-up bills.

Mom has no real need for cash, and she loses the purse at least once an hour. But on her insistence we see to it that she has a few dollars to keep, almost as playthings. She takes the bills from the purse, counts them and replaces them. Frequently.

As I stood to leave, she started unrumpling the bills and counting. I protested helplessly, as usual to no avail. Mom is very hard of hearing now, but she was always deaf to these entreaties. Finally, she counted out three dollars. She put the remaining two back in the purse. Then she changed her mind, took out another dollar and added it to the roll she was handing me. "Mom!" I exclaimed.

"Take it," she said. "I'm sorry. I didn't prepare any meals. Go take the family for corned beef." It wouldn't buy much corned beef. But apparently it bought her some satisfaction.

We kissed goodbye. Then, while Mom's attention was diverted, I stuffed the four bucks back into the purse. She would not remember having given them to me, I knew. And she'd have something to give me the next time.

Jan. 15, 1998

KEN STARR MEETS HIS MATCH

Poor Monica Lewinsky. What must it be like to have your mother interrogated by Kenneth Starr about your, uh, sexual indiscretions. What, I shudder to imagine, if it happened to ME?

STARR: Mrs. Frymer, you understand we want the truth and the whole truth about your son.

MOM: Well, Mr. Starr, he's a beautiful boy. I'm not just saying that because I'm his mother. You can ask anybody.

STARR: We're not concerned about his appearance, Mrs. Frymer. We are concerned with what he may have told you about his private life.

MOM: Listen, my son tells me everything. He calls me every Sunday, except when he's busy and he forgets. He didn't call already for a month. But, he's a very busy man. A journalist!!

STARR: Are you trying to tell me, Mrs. Frymer, that you do not know of the sort of life your son has led, with whom he associates?

MOM: What are you talking? Of course, I know. I'm his mother! It's just that lately he's been busy. You know he writes in a newspaper, like Walter Winchell.

STARR: And what does he do when he's not writing? Has he not confided in you, Mrs. Frymer?

MOM: What does he do? He's such a fine person he probably does a lot of charity. He gives to his temple. That's how I raised my children. They all have big hearts.

STARR: What has he confided?

MOM: Well, let me tell you, Mr. Prosecutor, he tells me that he is going to come visit the next time we have a holiday. He always thinks about me. On Mother's Day, he sent me a beautiful plant. It died, but I think I gave it too much water. It died, like, in a week.

STARR: Does he mention sex?

MOM: My son never uses dirty words. That's how I raised my children. He wouldn't use such a word. You know it took him a long time to get married. He was very particular. I used to tell him you can't be so particular, you're not getting younger. Thank God, he met this very lovely girl. I like her very much.

STARR: Who else has he met?

MOM: Who else? He's a married man! What do you mean who else?

STARR: That is what we are investigating, Mrs. Frymer.

MOM: Well, listen, big-shot prosecutor, you shouldn't say things like that. You have a dirty mind. Who else? God help me, who else? You should see his wife, what a lovely girl she is. She can make a brisket. Her house is spotless.

STARR: Your are deflecting the questions, Mrs. Frymer. It seems to me you are not a cooperative witness. I hope you understand the penalties associated with that.

MOM: Pardon me?

STARR: This is a serious matter, Mrs. Frymer. A serious matter. We are going to get to the bottom of this and we expect your cooperation.

MOM: Listen, you have to use smaller words. What did you say?

STARR: We want to know what your son has done!

MOM: Oh, God bless you, of course, I am glad you are interested in him. He has done such good things. He used to cut my lawn when he came to visit. I didn't want him to. He has a bad back. But that's the kind of person he is. I am glad you want to know. Listen, he used to win prizes in school. They gave him $50 once.

STARR: Mrs. Frymer! TELL THE COURT WHAT YOU KNOW!!

MOM: What are you shouting? Who raised you? I would like to talk with your mother! She should be ashamed the way you're yelling. My Murry never yells. Except when he gets nervous. But, listen, that happens. I don't complain.

STARR: Are you trying to pretend you know nothing?

MOM: Don't be such a smart guy, Mr. Prosecutor. I know lots of things. I used to have a job. I wasn't always in the house. What do you mean I know nothing? God help me, the way you talk. Bite your tongue.

STARR: The witness is excused. Please step down.

MOM: I'm going to tell my son what you said. You gave me such a headache I can't talk. Mr. Smart Guy. Who raised you???

Feb. 14, 1998

PEOPLE IN WAITING

I T WASN'T SO MANY YEARS AGO when, as a parent, a note from the principal might cause me worry. Now, it's a phone call from the administrator of the assisted living center in Ohio, and it's about Mom. Apparently, she's bugging some of the other residents, all in the 80–95 age group. Mom, who suffers from dementia, is 90.

As the administrator details the problem, Mom bothers the other (mostly) ladies, who prefer watching TV, which is what they do most of the day. I wince. Mom is merely following in my footsteps. In the third grade, I brought home a report card that said, to my chagrin, "Murry bothers girl in front of him too much."

Yes, I was, and still am, something of a botherer. Barb says so, too.

So now they are after Mom. I know why she is talking too much. She covets attention. That's a small problem in the third grade but intolerable when you're 90, in an institution where the staff is overworked and underpaid.

The worst part of the administrator's communique — as it would be from a school principal — is the suggestion that Mom should leave. He proposes a skilled nursing home. There's one next door, run by the same outfit. At about double the price. I shudder at the news. And I chat with the administrator. He says Mom needs more personal attention, more one-on-one.

Well, I've seen a lot of nursing homes, and personal attention is not their hallmark. Oh, yes, there are exceptions, but somehow I am not easy with the thought.

We had to move Mom out of her home nine months ago. We sold the house in which she raised us, fed us, gloried over us. We gave away her furniture, except for one bed and a dresser and a couple of chairs. They and Mom and her plants moved to the assisted living center. Now, instead of a house to rule, Mom has a tiny apartment. The plants, abhorring the change, all died.

The move was a shock to Mom, too, but we kept telling her it was for the best. She could not handle a house. She would have her own small place now, her meals would be served in a fancy dining room and she would have others with whom to share her days.

Mom stayed depressed for a long time. Then she broke her back and the healing was slow and painful. It seemed to me lately that she might be coming around, feeling a bit more comfortable. But Mom does not go silently into that good night. She wants attention. Yeah, Mom takes after me. And that is what adds to my consternation.

In the nursing home, Mom would share a room with another woman. The last few pieces of her furniture will be gone. Her once bustling kitchen, now a mere stove-less kitchenette, will be gone too. A busy, overworked staff will talk to her when they have time, but they have so much to do.

Yes, there is the guilt. Mom should be with her kids, but it is a daunting task now, beyond our abilities. Yet I know that if our roles were reversed, as once they were, Mom would devote each minute of each day giving care and finding it tolerable. When my father was dying with cancer, she sat with him day and night through agonizing months. There was no other way.

Now she is at the mercy of strangers. Her husband is gone. And her kids are stricken with the pain of their own helplessness. What to do? It's a common problem these days and it will get worse. More of us will live into our 90s, grow deaf, suffer with dementia and depression and, worst of all, loneliness. We have not yet really turned our attention to this future. We place parents in profit-making institutions and hope for the best.

No, it's not right. Life may not offer a happy ending, but our final days should be more than a withering wait for death.

March 24, 1998

ONE WORD: INFOSEEK

I HATE GETTING THOSE UNSOLICITED PHONE CALLS trying to sell me something. I seem to get them every day. I tell the caller to buzz off. But these jerks are persistent and sometimes you have to hang up on them.

For example, about a week ago, while I was taking a pleasant nap, I was awakened by a call from one of those Wall Street boiler rooms. "Have I got a stock for you!" this raspy-voiced character was saying, or some such. I quickly said that I was not interested and that I didn't buy stocks from raspy-voiced strangers I didn't know. But he persisted. He had a sure winner, he said. The stock was going to double, he said.

I said to buzz off. I said even worse than that. I said to take my name out of his file. I said to blow it out his ear. I said that if he didn't hang up, I would.

But he wouldn't quit. "Listen," he said. "Just listen. I have a stock that is going through the roof. Maybe double in a week."

"Sure," I said. "Sure. Then why don't you buy it?"

"Oh," he said. "I have. A thousand shares. But now I want to let you in on the deal, Mr. Frymer. This is a sure thing."

Well, I could see that the guy was not going to give up easily. "I'm going to hang up," I said. Sad to say, I'm such a wimp that even when being pushed, I stay polite. The salesman seemed to sense I was at the end of my tolerance.

"OK," he said. "I'll tell you. Listen. Infoseek. That's the stock. It's going through the roof. Do you know what Infoseek does?"

As a matter of fact, I do. It's a Santa Clara company and it's right here on my computer. I use it every once in a while to check on Internet things, including my stocks, which, given my pattern of hapless choices, usually go nowhere. Yes, indeed, I do know Infoseek. But it seemed to me, from something I remember reading in the business pages, that Infoseek was a bummer. It wasn't making money.

But I wasn't going to give this creep the benefit of a discussion. Yes, I told him, I know Infoseek and no, I told him, I wasn't interested. And then I hung up.

Sometimes when you hang up, the creep calls back and makes a derogatory comment, but this guy apparently had other fish to fry so I didn't hear from him again. But I was proud of myself for having sent him on his way. Still, just out of curiosity, I did check to see how Infoseek was doing. I was hoping it would tank.

The first day I checked, I noted that Infoseek had actually risen a couple of points. But that was due, I was sure, to the fact that stocks like Yahoo and America Online, which were in the same business, were flying high. So, I guess Joe Boiler Room was feeling cocky for a day. But two points do not a hot stock make, I comforted myself.

The next day Infoseek was up again. And the day after, again. Four points, I think. And on Thursday it zoomed, before finally sliding back on Friday. Still, the stock had nearly doubled in a week! Impossible! I had always known better than to take a tip from a nameless salesman who was calling at random. Impossible! But, yet, I could have made a couple of grand on a hundred shares of Infoseek if I had bitten. And I had hung up on him.

Well, you know what's going to happen, don't you? This guy is going to call again. He's going to cackle about how I didn't listen to him on Infoseek. Then he'll recommend another stock and say much the same thing. That it will double in a week. And I will actually ponder the bait. And then, remembering Infoseek, I ... might ... bite.

Sure, and then I will watch it sink, sink like the Titanic, out of sight. Yes, that is what is going to happen. And yet I feel somehow, sadly, hopelessly unable to prevent it. I am caught in the web now. What if the creep is right again?

April 18, 1998

FOND MEMORIES
OF THE GOOD OLD DAYS

I HAVE REACHED THAT FINE OLD AGE when, by law, I am supposed to tell the younger generations just how tough I had it in my youth. Regrettably, I have discovered that just the opposite is true. I remember mostly the good stuff.

Yes, I know that we in the dark ages did not have Viagra or Diet Coke and the only thing low-fat was Twiggy. But we did have this:

◆ When we drove our Ramblers to the gas station, we did not get out, walk to the "pay first" counter and stand behind seven people who were buying lottery tickets for their entire office staff. No, try to imagine this: A friendly attendant came up to the car and asked you how much gas you wanted. He would pump. And while you waited, he offered to check the oil, the air in the tires, clean the windshield and make witty commentary, like "Hot enough for you?" (And the maps were free.)

◆ When you called the telephone company — there was only one telephone company — you heard a human, live voice ask you what you wanted. I tried calling MCI yesterday on a billing matter, and after a half-dozen strolls through endless menus of "press one or two or three" choices, inevitably reached the big finish — "All our representatives are busy." I think all of MCI's representatives are vacationing in Bermuda and I anxiously await their return.

◆ There was some relationship between the pleasures of driving advertised in TV commercials and reality. Now, TV ads are the only place in the world that highways are clear; driving is pure pleasure; and the car never needs washing. In our brave new world, we get gang graffiti on overpasses and sometimes covering the road signs. And all the garbage along the side of the road? You can't get that on TV.

◆ In the old days in California, it never rained after April 1, and lovers were encouraged to shower together to save water. Now, of course, it never stops raining and disease-conscious lovers have a lot more to worry about than drought.

◆ You could buy your first home right after marriage, expecting to pay about two to three times your annual salary while the wife stayed home and baked cookies. Now in some rambunctious corners of our universe, if you, your wife, your kids, your mother, your dad and your pet dog can find good-paying jobs, you can buy your first house just prior to retirement, paying what used to be the national debt for a fixer-upper.

◆ The gang down at the office all got hired right out of college and worked in congenial camaraderie until getting their gold watches. And maybe the "old man," as he shook your hand, worried that you were breaking up "the family." Now you work for a multi-national corporation whose annually increasing profits are dependent on firing (downsizing!) everyone over 40. And that's when things are good.

◆ Yes, once upon a time sexual harassment meant your wife had a headache and political correctness meant you should vote on Election Day. And a sports utility vehicle was your rented golf cart. And the only place you could find a Web site was on a duck and TV news shows weren't restricted to lawyers arguing, two from the "right" and two from the "left."

Not that I'm actually nostalgic for days when populations were all homogeneous, gays stayed in the closet, the "ideal" women were mommies or Playboy bunnies, and Ed Sullivan was considered an entertainer. No, I guess we have made some gains.

But doggone it, I went to see the new "Titanic" the other day, and they left out Clifton Webb!

May 7, 1998

TIRES, TAXES AND
THE TWILIGHT ZONE

My MISSION WAS TO GET NEW TIRES for my car. I
drove to a neighborhood tire dealer and pulled my auto into
the small lot next to the store, got out, went in. The salesman
was a nice young man. He said he would accompany me outside and check out my tires.

"Where is your car?" he asked.

"Right there," I started to say. Except I didn't see it.
Strange, but I sometimes misplace where I've parked the car. I
looked around, all through the small lot. No car.

"Where?" he asked. "I don't know," I said. "I just parked it
a couple of minutes ago."

"In this lot?" he asked.

"My car has been stolen!" I blurted. "Somebody stole it in
two minutes! How could that happen?"

The nice young man seemed unconvinced, but he played
along. "Did you leave the keys in it?" he asked.

"I'm holding the keys," I said and showed him to prove it.
"And I locked it. I remember locking it. I definitely locked it.
How could somebody steal my car in two minutes right out-
side your door?"

The young man must have been wondering what my scam
was as we headed back inside. But then, just as I was heading
back through the door, I saw, out on the road, driving by, was

MY CAR! "There it is!" I yelled. "That's my car!!" I started to run toward the road to catch the thief. But the thief was apparently undaunted. He turned the car and headed right for me, into the lot, past me and toward the garage.

Then he got out, looking innocent, wondering why I was coming his way in such a hurry, waving my arms. "That's my car!" I said. "How did you manage to take it?"

The fellow was a mechanic at the tire dealer's. He was holding a set of keys, keys that fit my car but, apparently, belonged to another car of the same model, same year, that I suddenly noticed in the lot. Different color.

"Amazing," I said. "I never knew car keys from one car could fit another."

The salesman shrugged and told the mechanic to check license plates from now on. I shrugged and wondered what might have happened if I hadn't seen my car drive by. I might be talking to the police right now while tires I didn't order were being placed on the car. So, subdued, I headed home with a good story for the wife.

At home I noticed a letter had arrived from the IRS. It was thick. The bad kind.

It told me that the IRS would not deal with the woman who had written them on my behalf. It also said that they had rechecked my form and that my excuse over the inaccuracies were not acceptable.

What woman? I did not know the name of the woman who had written them on my behalf! What inaccuracies? I was aware of no inaccuracies. In fact, the letter dealt with issues I had never heard of before.

I called the IRS. After some wait, I reached an agent who asked me if I had written to the IRS. Yes, I had, some months earlier, but it was about an estimated payment and not at all about what the IRS had responded to. The agent checked a code number on the letter.

"Just write us and say this letter doesn't apply to you," she said without too much concern.

"But this has my Social Security number, my name. Will this mess up my taxes?" "Just send it back," the woman said.

"How could you answer one person's letter with a response to another problem? How did the two names get switched?"

"Just send it back," the agent repeated. And I hung up.

Then I heard my wife's car pull up to the house. I heard the garage door open. I heard her unlock the door to the house. I heard her voice calling to me. I did not move.

I was having a Twilight Zone day, and I had no idea who would be coming through that door.

Aug. 25, 1998

NEIGHBORS AND STRANGERS

As a typical urban dweller here in fast-growing Silicon Valley, I don't get to know most of my neighbors well. I plead guilty to not making the effort I should. Days and months and years fly by. There is an occasional nod, a passing wave at the curb when the weekly garbage is being placed. Maybe even a word or two now and then. Years pass.

I've lived in my home for the past 19 years. Thanks to Proposition 13, my neighborhood has proved to be rather stable. Most of my neighbors were there when I moved in.

One family, long-time residents, put their house up for sale a few weeks ago. And that is how we met, sort of, for the first time. I dropped in during an open house because I'd heard that their home was such a pretty place. And it was. It had all sorts of touches that I like, all reminiscent of the eastern United States, once my home.

And so I and my neighbors finally met, and talked, and found common interests, interests that had gone undiscovered for the 19 years. It is a lovely house and in today's market I assumed it would sell fast. The husband and wife living without children in the home were returning to Massachusetts, once my old stamping grounds. They were moving to be close to one of their now-married children and her family. There were grandkids back there.

Anyway, I and my new-found, soon-to-be-lost neighbors talked and found things in common. It was nice to hear they read this column. We were shown around the house and the lovely yard. Many of the touches were exquisite. We shared a few memories of other cities, other times. And then Barb and I left, talking to each other about the lovely home and the pleasant neighbors and what we had in common.

As I expected, the home sold fairly quickly, at a good price, too. I heard that my neighbors had been able to purchase a home in Massachusetts at half the price. Twice the house, too.

There was a garage sale and a few more moments of chat. My, how many people stop by when you are discarding old knickknacks. Cars were parked all over the street. Plants and tables and artwork and sundry other things were carted off by all sorts of people. The bargains were clearly irresistible. I didn't have a chance to chat again with my new-found longtime neighbors. Everything was moving fast.

One very early morning last week, before sun-up, while I was out picking up my newspaper, I noted that my neighbors were bustling in their lighted motor home. I wanted to wave, but I was wearing my robe, so I stared briefly in silence.

I guessed they might be leaving. It was too early to just be doing ordinary stuff. I went back into my house with the newspaper. The next time I looked out the window, the motor home was gone. The driveway was empty.

Nice people, I thought. I wish I had known them better and earlier. Later in the day, as I was getting home, I saw lots of activity at the house. There were cars parked in front and three male teenagers were playing basketball in the driveway. I thought to myself that I hoped these new people weren't unusually noisy or anything like that.

I went into my house, thinking again for a moment of the

previous family, who had lived in their home for almost 25 years, who were on some highway somewhere heading to Massachusetts, whom I wish I had known better.

Ah, well. I think my street will be undergoing rapid change. Many of the residents are older. There are few children around and this was meant to be a family neighborhood. Over at the neighborhood pool, I know hardly anyone now. My neighbors are younger and they are raising young families. My own kids have long since moved away.

I wish I had known my old neighbors better. Apparently my sons and one of their sons had a passing acquaintanceship many years back. Ah, well. I probably won't get to know the new people since we are of such disparate generations. And I am an old-timer on a changing street.

July 21, 1998

THE SCHMOOZE FACTOR

THE ELDERLY WOMAN ahead of me in the bank line wanted to talk. To the teller, to me, to anybody. She said she didn't get out as much as she used to. She said things had changed around here. I nodded. The bank teller was busy.

"Sorry to keep you waiting," the teller told the woman.

"That's OK," the woman said brightly at the sound of a human voice. "I'm 76. I've got lots of time."

The white-haired woman was dressed in a frilly white blouse and skirt. I wondered if I should tell the woman I admired her blouse, but I decided against it. Frankly, it might lead to more conversation than I could handle at that moment. But I remember how carefully my own mother used to pick her clothes for "going out" to the bank. It would be nice, I used to think, if someone admired my mother's blouse on those days.

Nowadays, of course, casual compliments are rare because human contact is rarer. The voice on the telephone is recorded. (My mother usually fails to realize this and starts telling the voice about her hearing problems. She gets disconnected.)

Lots of times I feel equally disconnected. Society has managed to drain itself of what we used to call "shmoozing," i.e. idle conversation. Maybe not in shmooze capitals like New York. But suburbia is especially deprived.

For one thing, we are all locked away in our own private

chariots as we move about from place to place. For human voices, we try the radio. It's not the same. It's Dr. Laura yelling at some poor caller who, like many of us, just wants to shmooze.

I used to chat with the postal carrier, but recently we seem to have a different postal carrier every day. The young woman carrier who was familiar on my route, waving as she went by, is long gone. I liked her.

Even the bank tellers seem to last but a few months. Not that bank telling (is that the word?) is lifetime work. But I liked it when I became familiar with a face or two.

Some people get to shmooze at work, though employers think that a waste of time and productivity. Employees are increasingly isolated in cubicles to keep them working. It probably does help the bottom line, though it does terrible things to the head.

I know some people who do all their shmoozing on the computer. They join chat rooms and talk to Chinese peasants and Norwegian businessmen. That's not a bad thing, if looking into faces, hearing laughter or patting an arm doesn't matter.

I think the elderly, like that woman at the bank, are the most distressed by this state of affairs. The elderly and little children have much in common. They crave attention. They like to touch. They are very concerned with establishing identities, because, unlike us working types, they have few places to do it.

I feel kind of sorry for tots. They look up at you at the supermarket with quizzical expressions, looking to broaden their universe. I want to reach out and pat a little head, but then there is a lot of suspicion when older folks play with unrelated little kids. I guess that, under the circumstances of our times, that is right. But a terrible loss, nonetheless.

Our lives have been radically limited. Television, computers and cars have combined to separate each of us. And in automobile-dominated areas of the country, it is worse because all the potential shmoozees are inside their cars and you can't check them out, even visually.

So we don't meet as many people as we used to, and we don't shmooze as much as we used to. Now I don't want to make a big thing of this, but I'll bet that our national mental health is somehow affected by our isolation.

This curiosity about others and how they interact may be why we find President Bill and intern Monica so fascinating. No, come to think of it, their encounter deals with another human need entirely.

Still, Bill is in terrible trouble not only because of the sex, but because Monica, like so many of us, had this inexorable need to call Linda and shmooze.

Aug. 27, 1998

THE NURSING HOME

Mom was on the floor when they found her. She didn't know when or if she had fallen. She did know that she had an awful pain in her lower back.

The people at the assisted-living home near Cleveland, where Mom has lived for the past 15 months, took her to the hospital, where X-rays revealed nothing. But she said she was in terrible pain, so she remained in the hospital. Her first night, she got up to go to the bathroom and fell again. The next day, the hospital placed a night nurse at her bedside to watch over her. I got to the hospital a few days later. Mom looked wan and drugged, but mostly she was upset. Actually, that wasn't a bad sign. When you're 91, getting upset takes a certain amount of spunk, and Mom has always had that in abundance. She complained about the treatment she was getting. They had not given her so much as a piece of bread, she said.

I spoke to the nurse, who said that while Mom initially refused her meals, she would nibble on them if they were left by her side, and that eventually she'd eat most of the meal. When lunch arrived during my visit, she said she wasn't hungry and insisted I eat it.

Mom wanted out of bed, but found it too painful. Maybe tomorrow. But she wanted out of the hospital today. She wanted to go home to her house. Mom has forgotten she has no house now. And the one home she does have, the assisted-living center, said she could no longer return because she needed more care than they could provide. So the hospital bed was, for the moment, home. Mom, distraught, suspected that.

Conversations with Mom have grown increasingly difficult over the years. Her deafness, and her refusal to wear a hearing aid, is one problem. Her dementia, now made worse by the new circumstances of the hospital, is another.

My younger sister, who has always lived near our mother, has provided her with care and attending concern over the years since Dad died. I moved away as a young man. Mom now confuses her dutiful daughter with her own mother and sometimes speaks to her as such. But when I show up, there is no confusion. "This is my son!" my mother tells the nurses and the aides and the cleaning women and the passing orderlies, showing exaggerated pride. I try to shush her to no avail.

"You are the boss now," my mother declares.

"Why aren't I the boss?" my sister taunts. My mother waves her off.

Then my sister and I must go off looking for a nursing home that might have a vacancy. They are not easy visits. The residents, sitting together, but isolated nevertheless, stare as we pass. They seem desperately alone and unhappy. One man in a wheelchair, his face hollowed, follows us to the door and says he wants out, he wants to go with us. We cannot dissuade him. Is he mentally ill or simply saying what I would say in his situation?

Back at the hospital, a new X-ray has discovered that, indeed, there is a fracture in Mom's tailbone. She is in great pain. She says she wants to die. Then she pleads that we not abandon her. But when told it is the Jewish New Year, Mom begins a benediction of good wishes. "Families are the most important thing," she says. "You should always look out for one another. You are my whole life. I want to live."

After a few days of visits, I must go back to California. We have found a nursing home that will take Mom, though, of course, there are concerns about the care she will receive. It is so easy to mistreat the elderly. Few listen to them.

At the airport, I call Mom one more time to say goodbye. But Mom knocks the phone to the floor, out of reach. I can hear her calling the nurse, saying that the phone has just rung and someone must be on the line. The nurse, irritable, tells my mother that she has imagined it, that the phone has not rung.

I keep yelling, "Hello! Hello!," into the mouthpiece but the nurse does not hear me. My mother begs that someone answer the phone. The busy nurse tells her to be still. Moments later, feeling helpless and distressed, I get on a plane that will fly me away.

Sept. 26, 1998

THE DAY OF ATONEMENT

W<small>HEN I WAS A BOY</small>, the Day of Atonement was a really scary event. It had been impressed on me that it was on the Day of Atonement (Yom Kippur) that God determined the Book of Life, inserting therein who would live and who would die in the ensuing year.

Since the day was one of fasting, I refused so much as brushing my teeth for fear of swallowing a little water, thereby angering my God and getting left out of the book. Of course, I would reason with myself that drinking a little water could not possibly be as big a sin as, say, the ones Hitler had committed and somehow he was still (at that time) in the book year after year.

Just how was this list determined, I wondered. Were you de-listed because of a your persistent snubbing of commandments or did the inherent goodness or badness in your heart count?

When I was young, such questions, and the matter of life and death itself, were a source of constant musing. For example, when an airplane crashed and 150 people died, did those 150 happen to have all been placed on that plane for some reason that I did not know but that God did? And how did he manage to get them all together to take that trip?

When I walked on the sidewalk and stepped on some ants,

were the ones I stepped on evil and were the ones I missed good? And what did my elders mean when they said that "only the good die young"? That flew in the face of the lessons of the Day of Atonement.

Of course, the big underlying question was: How did God decide? And what could I do to influence his thinking?

Well, tonight's the beginning of the Jewish Day of Atonement, and while I don't mull these things the way I used to, I am still concerned. I do not like to believe that life and death are mere accidents, such as taking the right plane or not crossing the street when a car goes out of control. I want to believe that how one lives his or her life is meaningful in how long one gets to live. But then I cannot believe that the hundreds of thousands of babies killed in the Holocaust were guilty of anything. And I have been shocked to learn over the years how long many of the Nazi perpetrators lived, comfortably, in places like Argentina or Germany or even the United States.

It may be that God rights these things in the afterlife with heaven and hell. I certainly hope so. But I don't know, and it is by no means assured where I might be sent.

What I want most is to know that God pays attention. Maybe the wrong people succeed and the right people fail. Maybe some bad people live happier lives than some good people. The important thing is that God knows this, that he pays attention. If God pays attention, then there is all manner of correction possible. It may be heaven and hell, or it may be something far more intricate that mortals could never figure out.

I do believe, though, that what you do on this Earth matters, that there is a pay back in one way or another. As I have grown from childhood to more advanced age, I have accumulated all sorts of evidence that this may not be the case, but it is inconceivable to me that God doesn't care.

It is just that I do not always see it. Or that the pure of heart are rewarded by dint of that purity and that the evil ones among us suffer in some way that is not always apparent.

I think it is the function of all religions to assure us of such things. We flounder through our days, reasoning that certain actions bring certain results. Religion tells us that the choices we make are critical, that someday, somehow, some way, we will learn of that certainty.

But you have to believe. Life sometimes seems to produce results that fly in the face of what ought to be! You have to believe. And I do. And so I pray this night that those I love are written into the book, for they are good people. And I pray that my own compromises, my occasional insensitivity, the hurts I have given others, are forgiven.

And, dear reader, may you, too, be written into the Book of Life. I need you and am willing to overlook your flaws, if only you will do the same.

Sept. 29, 1998

DO I LIVE HERE?

"Do I live here?" my mother asks me when I visit her at the Cleveland nursing home where she now resides. It's a wretched question, but I try to smile and answer "yes."

"Do you like it here?" I ask, but she doesn't understand what I mean, nor do I.

Mom is 91 and suffers from dementia, among other maladies. She maintained her own house until last year, but it was no longer safe for her, despite home nursing care. Since then, we — her guilt-ridden, aging offspring — have had to move her far too many times as we search for some acceptable place for her final years, or months, or days.

She has been to an assisted living center, but they discarded her in months, claiming she needed a nursing home. She has been to the hospital twice, for broken bones. She has been to a combined assisted living center-nursing home, but she hated it there and so did we. Now Mom is in an expensive "home," considered desirable. There is a waiting list. Medicaid picks up the tab for most residents, including a surprising number of recent immigrants. Mom, who has lived a penurious life, still has some savings, so she pays her own way.

The home, with its religious observance, seems pleasant, even festive, during the holidays. But Mom wears an alarm taped to an ankle. Nurses complain she tries to remove it.

The outside doors are locked.

Most of the aged residents, primarily women, appear passive, even vacant, as they sit in the TV room or the game room or the dining room or the discussion room, where Mom is sitting when we arrive. A staffer is leading a discussion on, of all things, the Clinton affair and the Iraq bombings. No one responds. Many are asleep, slumped awkwardly in wheelchairs or on sofas.

Mom is taken by surprise, delighted to see Barb and me. She is all dressed up in a new outfit, her hair is coiffed and her nails are polished. I am pleased. Mom looks good.

But after the early greetings, the talk wears on her and she gets confused easily. She is quite deaf. She cannot remember anything beyond the moment. Each visit begins like "Groundhog Day," a brand-new repetition of the same conversation.

As pleasant as the place appears, with its holiday decorations, a visiting children's choir, even a staff puppy, it is difficult to linger. These are people who are not getting better. They have been stored here by spouses and offspring who find home care beyond their abilities.

One old man sits talking softly to a wife who is asleep. Others visit in family groups, speaking mostly to each other as Grandma or Grandpa looks on silently. We want out, so we take Mom to lunch one day at her favorite restaurant. She seems pleased, but as usual, she insists on paying. But she has nothing in her worn purse but some cookies. I put a dollar in and tell her she has paid for lunch. She says it is wonderful to be with her family, but she can't remember who is who.

Back at the nursing home, she shares a room with a Russian woman, a recent immigrant. They have virtually no communication.

All the rooms have little biographies of their residents pasted outside the walls. I walk up and down the hall reading them. Most are quite brief. A name, an age and then: "Mother of Rosalie and Debbie." It seems more like an epitaph than a bio. Another biography says only: "Was a truck driver." Nothing else.

However, directly across from Mom's room is a lengthy bio of a man with "Dr." in front of his name. He was a psychologist until 1995 and a few years before that had been the chairman of the psychology department at Yale. He is 86. I am awed and peer into the room. An aged, frail man in a robe sits reclining awkwardly in front of his TV set. I sigh at the sight. Mom has had no education at all. This man is a Ph.D., who has written important books. Old age is a great leveler.

After most of a week, we come to say our goodbyes. We mention California, unsure if Mom understands we live far away. She thanks us for the visit, then tearfully hunts through her ragged purse, comes up with a dollar and a cookie.

Dec. 29, 1998

CAN'T WE JUST GET ALONG?

I HAD A TERRIBLE HEADACHE and the plane was delayed. It was oversold. We were offered $500 vouchers to get off, but I didn't want to hunt for a hotel room. Finally, after 45 minutes, we took off on a six-hour flight to San Jose. Maybe I could sleep.

But then I felt this strong poking in my back. Maybe the guy behind me was fiddling with his tray table. No, it continued. It felt like kicks.

Finally, despite my usual timidity in situations of confrontation, I twisted in my seat to see who was poking me. All I could see was the top of a little head. A child was kicking the rear of my seat. "Pardon me, madam," I said to the woman reading a magazine in the seat beside the child. "Your son is kicking the back of my seat."

I figured that should do it. Her apology was not necessary. Instead, the woman was offended. "He's only a child," she said.

"Yes," I agreed. "But he's kicking the back of my seat." I really didn't know what to say next. It was not something I could discuss with someone else's child.

"I can't get him to stop," the woman replied curtly. "Maybe you could switch your seat."

My headache suddenly exploded as the blood rushed to my head. I should move my seat because she can't control her kid? I was flabbergasted. Still, fighting to maintain my composure, I said that the plane was full and I didn't think someone else would welcome sitting in my seat so long as her kid kept kicking.

The woman, wearying of my complaint, went back to her magazine. Her little son went back to his attack with a little more zest. And I pondered my options. I couldn't think of any. As my pounding continued, both in my head and on my back, I gave it one more shot and urged the mother to deal with the problem. But the other passengers were beginning to find me the problem now.

Oh, I did hear the mother make some feeble effort on my behalf, telling her son: "That mean man is real mad and he going to get you if you keep kicking him." The child, facing a real ogre now, kicked even harder. Stifling my rage, I tried to sleep. And eventually the child fell asleep, too. I survived. End of story, but not my complaint. I fear that I have become some sort of grumpy old man. The airplane incident was not unique.

In restaurants I have sat near children who were having tantrums while their parents missed not a beat in their conversation.

I have learned to be wary of sitting back-to-back in booths where rambunctious tots have eminent domain. Standing on the seat facing the neighboring booth is great fun. If the child is cute enough, it may well be fun for a moment or two, but this can last a meal. Ah, I fear I am losing those of you who have the unappreciated task of controlling bored offspring. It isn't easy. Maybe, as the woman on the plane suggested, it is I who should move. Maybe I'm going to the wrong restaurants.

Or maybe I have a terribly old-fashioned view of parenting. Kids can and do behave well when parents urge them to.

And if kids can't behave, should they be let out of the house?

I am grumpy, but I felt this way even when I was trying to control my own tots. It isn't kids who are the problem, but parents who imply they are not responsible for them. I see this insensitivity to others spreading. Is the teen on the beach blasting his stereo? Let those who are annoyed get up and leave.

The same holds at the movies. Noisy teens behind you? Don't even try to confront it. Move. And get out of the way on the highway if the other driver appears to dominate the road. Move quickly.

This is becoming a mighty crowded planet, where rubbing shoulders is unavoidable. As the great Rodney King put it so eloquently when his own highway journey ended badly: "Can't we all get along?"

Ah, there it is. That is what I should have said to the woman behind me on the plane. "Madam," I should have said, with a sigh, "Dear madam, can't we all get along?"

Well, no, it didn't work for King, either.

Jan. 7, 1999

MISTER CLEAN

I'M IN THE MOOD to throw things out. I sometimes get in this mood at 3 a.m., lying awake in bed and wondering what's gone wrong with my life. I want to get up and get rid of old books that I've had since college, old shirts I never wear, old rugs, old letters, old photos.

I have a collection of photos I took home after my mother moved out of her house. They were in the family photo album. But these aren't photos of me or my sister or our kids. These are pictures of people neither my sister nor I know, people from some other country who were friends or family or neighbors. Who knows? My mother no longer knows. I don't know. But I've saved the photos. Throw them out.

I have newspaper clippings of old shows I was involved in. They are torn and tattered and, as important as they were once upon a time, they are not important now. I want to get down to what is important now. The bare minimum. Throw them out.

I have books from my freshman year in college. Why in the world have I saved them so many years? Why have I carted them from house to house to house? What do these books mean to me anymore? Throw them out.

My clothes are the most pitiful part of my clutter. Sure, there are shirts in my closet that I've never worn, that are per-

fectly fine, that are top brand names. But the necks are tight
now and the styles may have changed, though I keep thinking
they will come back someday. Forget it. Let somebody the Sal-
vation Army knows wear them.

Ties? Don't ask. Toss.

Inevitably all this cleanup leads to a conflict with my wife.
Not that I want to toss her. She still has lots of good use left.
No, but she has collections of vegetarian magazines. Why
would anyone save 100 vegetarian magazines? How many
ways are there to slice carrots? Get rid of them, I say, but she
says hands off. It kills me. Doesn't she see the good I am ac-
complishing tossing and throwing and filling the garbage bags?
It is a feeling of cleanliness, of erasure, of new beginnings.

Throw away your own things, she says. Arrrggghhh!!

The garage is the most fertile territory for discards. We
have an old white dresser from the kids' bedroom that we
bought — I kid you not — when they were babies. My
youngest son has stuffed the drawers with term papers and the
like from his college days. Why is this jam-packed dresser alive
and well in my garage? I have to get rid of it!

Check with Ben, says Barb. It's my garage! I yell. ("Yell" indicates thoughtful debate in a slightly raised tone.) They're his
term papers, she says. He may be saving them for something.

It's this kind of interference that upsets my whole mood.
Don't you understand? I am cleaning house. I am renewing
my life. I will be a new man if only I can get rid of everything!

"Clean your own stuff" comes the persistent retort. It
grinds into my psyche. When one is cleaning one's house, one
cannot make exceptions. It is especially other people's stuff
that must go. To be the boss, one must toss. I head into the
closets. Old trophies. I cannot remember from where or why.
An old camera, perfectly good, never to be used again. Old

tapes. I can't remember what's on them.

Slowly, slowly, the fever begins to ebb. I grow weary. Do I want to eliminate my collection of sweatshirts from every college I ever visited? Do I want to throw away my Perry Como records?

The passion starts to die. Oh, yes, if I could get rid of those vegetarian magazines, it might rekindle, but I can't, so it starts to flame out. If I can't clean absolutely everything, then there is no point to this exercise. I may as well shut the closet doors, push the garage clutter to one side, put away the mystery photo album, and maybe get those old new shirts laundered. They will look better laundered.

I will reconsider the cleanup later, at some other 3 a.m., when I'm not so tired.

Feb. 4, 1999

TIME LEAVENS LOVE

I THINK WE MARRY when we find someone truly compatible. Handsome/beautiful is good. But compatibility sets us up for life. We marry when we find someone who thinks the way we do, who likes the same sort of movies, who eats her popcorn just the way you eat your popcorn (a little salt, no butter).

In a way, that is the true meaning of love. You like Sinatra; she likes Sinatra. You like ice cream; she likes ice cream. You like vanilla; she likes vanilla.

You marry the person who thinks the same way about who's funny and who's not. You marry the person who laughs at the same jokes you do and frowns at the same awful puns.

What a thrill it is to find that special person on some enchanted evening across a crowded room. You know at a glance. She is the one who shares your taste in novels and wants to listen to the same music. You are ready to go anywhere together for Gershwin.

And so, your heart beating madly, you run right out and buy the ring. And when your friends ask you why, you say because she shares all your attitudes and all your opinions and all your loves and all your hates. You dislike Nixon and she dislikes Nixon. You think Arthur Miller said it all in "Death of a Salesman" and so does she.

Your favorite little restaurant quickly becomes her favorite little restaurant. You like visiting the same stores in the same parts of town. An excursion to Switzerland is exactly what you both find the ideal vacation. No need to wonder, no questions to ask. You are breathlessly, happily compatible.

And then, of course, time passes. She's into food fads; you like fat foods. You begin yawning at 9, go to bed at 10. She likes to read her nights away, staying up till 1. You get up at 5. She sleeps till noon. (Eventually you hardly see each other.)

She likes movies where the heroine dies a tearful death from some mysterious disease. You like Clint Eastwood making his day. It's not easy finding something that you can see together, but you settle on whatever's close.

You laugh at Jay Leno. She wonders what the heck you're laughing at. You want your sons to grow up to be president (still) or Bill Gates. She wants them to grow up to be sensitive. You want your daughter to grow up to be president or marry Bill Gates. She wants her to be true to herself. (Who's that?)

Picking a restaurant is now a chore. She likes big salads. You like little salads, with prime rib and a couple of glasses of wine. How in the world, you wonder, can anyone watch a soap opera, unchanging, day after day? Why in the world, she wonders, would anyone watch basketball? All they do is drop a ball in a hole.

You try to tell her what you think, how you feel, what's ahead, what's behind. She tries to tell you what she thinks, how she feels, what's ahead, what's behind. You've both heard it all too many times before.

And how come her friends and your friends are from different planets? And how come holding hands at midnight 'neath a starry sky now sounds so impractical? Well, it's hard to stay up till midnight and it's cold 'neath a starry sky. All those opinions you shared now are more complex, and who in the world thinks the way she does?

And yet ...

Amazingly, you are more compatible than you were at first. There are things you like about her that you never knew back then. And she hangs around and keeps you company when the girl back then would have fled.

The arguments are comfortable because you know where you stand. And you have produced children together. And whoever they are, they are yours. And now love becomes familiarity. And familiarity brings understanding. And understanding brings warmth.

Time has changed everything. Lucky you. Lucky us.

Feb. 11, 1999

·

ACKNOWLEDGMENTS

Many people at the San Jose Mercury News helped in the writing of these columns. There are the usual suspects: feature editors and copy editors, research librarians and fellow writers. Publisher Jay Harris and Executive Editor David Yarnold gave the necessary support. Assistant managing editor Ann Hurst served as editor of this book, choosing and organizing the columns. Bob Drews was both a mentor and copy editor. The design and cover are the work of Bill Prochnow.

My family provided daily inspiration and graciously endured some loss of privacy. I am grateful.

And certainly I must thank the readers of the Mercury News and other newspapers around the country where the columns appeared for their nurturing response to my writing over the years. Their kindness and support were always the greatest reward.

Murry Frymer
September, 1999